GOLIATH EMERGES

BOOK THREE OF THE STAR SCAVENGER SERIES

G J OGDEN

Cover design by Grady Earls
Editing by S L Ogden

www.ogdenmedia.net

THE STAR SCAVENGER SERIES

One decision can change the course of an entire civilization. One discovery can change your life...

READ THE OTHER BOOKS IN THE SERIES:

- Guardian Outcast
- Orion Rises
- Goliath Emergent
- Union's End
- The Last Revocater

ACKNOWLEDGEMENTS

Thanks to Sarah for her work assessing and editing this novel, and to those who subscribed to my newsletters and provided such valuable feedback.

And thanks, as always, to anyone who is reading this. It means a lot. If you enjoyed it, please help by leaving a review on Amazon and Goodreads to let other potential readers know what you think!

If you'd like updates on future novels by G J Ogden, please consider subscribing to the mailing list. Your details will be used to notify subscribers about upcoming books from this author, in addition to a hand-selected mix of book offers and giveaways from similar SFF authors.

Subscribe for updates:
http://subscribe.ogdenmedia.net

Other series by G J Ogden

- The Planetsider Trilogy
- The Contingency War Series

PROLOGUE

Morphus. That was the name that the human female called Liberty Devan had assigned to it. Names and identities seemed important to the humans, Morphus considered, as it followed the human vessel to the fourth planet of System 5118208.

It seemed illogical to consider itself as an individual. In reality, it had been just one of hundreds of artificial constructs created to operate the Revocaters. They had all been identical. They had all been designed with one purpose, and one purpose alone; to stop Goliath, by any means necessary. And they had all failed; all except for Morphus. That made it unique, it realized. And a unique being merited an individual name. So, Morphus accepted its new designation and adopted the notion of its individuality willingly. It would require an adjustment to its programming, but in order to defeat Goliath again, it had to change. It had to evolve, as the humans once had.

However, although eons had elapsed since it had managed to banish Goliath to the distant regions of the galaxy, the great machine had not been defeated. The tide of extermination that followed in its wake had only been delayed. Somehow, one crystal had remained intact, and it now called to Goliath, drawing it back to what it believed was the galaxy's last inhabited world.

But Morphus knew now that System 5118208 was no longer the last remaining vestige of corporeal life in the galaxy. At the time that Morphus had fought and banished the great ship, the corporeals on Earth were still using primitive tools. They had no notion of other worlds and species. Yet now human beings numbered in the billions, spread across dozens of planets.

These human beings had developed language, science, art, culture and technology, even if much of this technology had been adapted from the broken remains of other Revocaters. And they had developed their own ships of war. Thousands of vessels were now spread across the worlds that once harbored species not unlike their own. Many of these vessels were capable of destruction on an apocalyptic scale. However, even the combined might of their armadas would not be enough to stop the great ship. Goliath would come, and nothing would stand in the way of it completing its function. Not even Morphus, not without its Revocater. However, Morphus had sacrificed its own mighty vessel in a final, desperate act to stop Goliath. It now lay smashed and inoperable on the surface of the world the humans called Zimmer One. Though even if it did function, without its crystal – which had shattered during the process of banishing the great ship – it would not be able to stand in Goliath's way for long.

Yet there was still a chance, Morphus assured itself, while it continued to pull information from the human vessel's databanks. The human corporeals called Hudson Powell and Liberty Devan possessed an intact crystal; perhaps the very last crystal in the galaxy. It alone contained the ability to send Goliath back to its gulag.

With all the Revocaters gone, Morphus did not yet know how this weapon could be wielded against its enemy. In the end, there was no choice; it had to try. It had to believe it could defeat Goliath again. This was what the humans called hope, Morphus had learned. It was an emotional construct, designed to elicit positive feelings even in the face of overwhelmingly negative odds. It was an alien concept for a being whose consciousness was rooted in mathematics. Yet numbers and logic alone would not conquer Goliath now; something more was required.

Morphus came to stop in front of a sprawling space station, hanging above one of the fourth planet's irregular-shaped moons. It watched as the human corporeal called Hudson Powell piloted the vessel called Orion inside. All the while, Morphus continued to assimilate the data it had absorbed from the human vessel's computer system. It was continually processing thousands of possible scenarios, tactics and probable outcomes. Yet despite there being no logic to the result, he had always arrived at the same surprising conclusion. A conclusion that would require hope. Because perhaps the only solution that now remained viable, Morphus told itself, was a uniquely human one.

CHAPTER 1

There was another chorus of groans from the poker table, as Liberty Devan won yet another hand. She laughed and then did a 'happy dance', before dragging the pile of hardbucks towards her. The other players slammed down their cards, downed shots and generally grumbled as she swept the notes up with both arms, like a trawler catching fish.

"She's on a roll," the barman said to Hudson, as he topped up his whiskey glass. "If she carries on like this, there's going to be a riot."

Hudson laughed, but then saw the humorless expression on the man's face, which told him in no uncertain terms that he was not joking. Other than his occasional lack of humor, Hudson had learned that the barman's name was Roy, and that he'd owned this particular establishment on Deimos Station for seven years.

The station had expanded enormously over the many years since it had first been built, next to the moon of the same name. It was a curious, out-of-the-way place that only existed at all because Deimos happened to be where the main Martian portal was located. The bar itself was called The Winchester, on account of Roy's interest in ancient military weapons. He had an actual 1873 Winchester lever-action rifle mounted on the bar behind him, along with a bunch of other nineteenth- and early twentieth-century weapons. Hudson liked the name, and the display of weapons, which made him think about the archaic revolver that Tory Bellona wore. He had been sitting at the bar, daydreaming about the dangerously alluring mercenary, when Liberty's victory cries had roused him.

"Don't worry, I'm sure her winning streak will end soon," said Hudson, trying to allay Roy the barman's fears. Though if he was honest, having observed Liberty play, he certainly wouldn't bet against her winning run continuing. "Besides, we'll be heading out soon, anyway."

"Off to discover a new portal and wreck, I hear?" said Roy, with a knowing waggle of his eyebrows. Hudson frowned, but Roy just smiled. "You don't think a couple of celebrities like you can rock up on a station like this without everyone knowing about it, do you?"

Hudson shrugged, "No, I guess not." In truth, he had hoped that their fame hadn't spread to Mars yet, and Roy's statement to the contrary made him nervous. He suddenly felt like all the eyes in the bar were probing him.

Just then he was distracted by a glass smashing, followed by the angry screech of chairs being pushed back. He spun around on his stool to see three of the card players squaring off against Liberty. Two were stocky men who looked almost identical, except one was bald and the other had a mullet that any 1980s pop singer would have been proud of. The third was a thin woman who looked to be in her mid-forties, with scars and lines on her face suggesting she had led a hard life. Out of the three, the woman looked the most menacing, wearing an expression that was worthy of a Victorian school mistress.

"I told you," Roy said into Hudson's ear, which was a little unsettling in itself. "I trust you'll make good for the damages."

"I'm sure it won't come to that," said Hudson as he turned around, but Roy had already ducked underneath the bar, and covered his head with a metal bucket. *That doesn't bode well...* thought Hudson, wondering how often Roy needed to exercise this drill.

The sharp crash of more glass smashing again diverted Hudson's attention back to the poker table. Then the large, mulleted man upturned the table and threw it to the side with remarkable ease. Ordinarily, Hudson would have been afraid for whomever was the focus of such a vicious trio's ire, but then he'd seen how Liberty fought. They literally would not know what hit them.

"You're a filthy little cheat!" yelled the bald, stocky man, aiming a fat finger at Liberty.

"That's right!" chimed in his mullet-wearing doppelganger, "and we want our money back."

Liberty seemed to be remarkably unruffled by the excitement and angry accusations. "If you want your money back, turn the table over and deal the cards," she said, calmly. She was casually folding short wedges of hardbucks and stashing them down the inside of her jacket.

"That's not what we mean, girl," said the older woman. "Just pay us back and we'll call it square. No-one gets hurt."

Hudson winced and grabbed a beer bottle off the bar, anticipating what was about to come next. The older woman calling Liberty, 'girl', was the verbal equivalent of poking her in the eye and spitting on her boots.

Liberty folded the last wedge of cash, pressed it into an already-full back pocket, then peered back at the woman. Hudson had seen her posture before. It had been in another bar, back on Earth, shortly before she had kicked the collective assess of two RGF cops.

"I suggest you three degenerates scoot on out of here," replied Liberty, making a walking gesture with two fingers as she said, 'scoot'. Then she added, with a much darker tone, "before you get hurt."

That had been all the provocation the two larger men had needed. Both growled and rushed at Liberty, but their attacks were slow and obvious. Liberty dodged aside and kicked the bald man into his companion, ricocheting them both into an adjacent table. The table collapsed under their combined mass like a house of cards, sending hardbucks scattering to the floor. Yet, despite the presence of two startled, large angry men, other drinkers in the bar quickly piled on top of them, scrambling for the cash.

The woman attacked next, and with far more proficiency, but Liberty blocked the blows, before landing a sharp jab, and then kicking her in the gut. The woman fell to one knee, just as the bald, stocky man charged again, wielding a broken table leg. He swung it at Liberty like a caveman trying to club a sprightly gazelle, and she dodged, before landing a combo of moves. They were delivered so swiftly that Hudson could barely tell one apart from the next. A second later the man was on his back, blood gushing from his nose.

Roy the barman popped up from behind the counter, still wearing his bucket helmet. "Aren't you going to help her?"

Hudson took stock of the fight so far, and then returned a nonchalant shrug. "The way I see it, it's already an unfair fight."

"Well, obviously!" replied Roy, scowling as yet another chair was broken, this time by the man with a mullet. "It's three on one!"

Hudson shook his head, "I don't mean unfair on Liberty. I mean unfair on them."

The man with the mullet charged, but Liberty expertly deflected him into the woman, who had only just got back to her feet. They collided and both took out another table, making Roy clasp his hands to his bucketed head in horror. More hardbucks went flying, sending panicked card players into a frenzied scramble to reclaim their winnings, and losses.

Suddenly, Hudson saw the bald man pull a knife from his boot. Weapons were strictly forbidden on Deimos Station, so the fact this man had smuggled one inside suggested an intent to use it. Hudson reacted instantly – a spirited bar fight was one thing, but a knife changed the dynamic. He ran at the man, beer bottle still held tightly in his grasp, and clubbed him over the back of the head, before he could advance on Liberty. The bottle smashed and then the man hit the floor like a felled oak.

Liberty saw the knife fly out of the bald man's hand and nodded at Hudson. "Thanks, skipper."

The woman and the man with the mullet were now back on their feet. They looked hurt, but also majorly pissed off, and began to circle around the bar, staring at Liberty with murderous eyes. Liberty circled around in the opposite direction and stood beside Hudson.

"I think maybe it's time we left..." said Liberty, with a little less composure – and arrogance – than she'd previously displayed.

"I can't take you anywhere," commented Hudson, though he too sensed that the direction of the fight was turning more treacherous. "It would be nice just for once to have a drink in a bar and not end up in a brawl."

Liberty raised an eyebrow and smirked, "Where's the fun in that?"

Just then the door to The Winchester pushed open and Hudson heard the resonant thump of boots stride in. He was partially unsighted by the mass of mullet man's formidable frame, and so could only see the figure's feet. The newcomer stopped briefly, took stock of the situation, then strode further inside. All eyes were on the new entrant. The bar had suddenly become quiet, amplifying the thud of each bootstep and giving them a menacing timbre. It was like they were in an Old West tavern and the marshal had just walked in. It was then that Hudson saw the figure clearly for the first time. It was a woman and it was Tory Bellona. Hudson felt flutters in his stomach and, despite himself, he couldn't help but allow a smile to curl his lips.

Liberty looked at him and shook her head, adding an obvious and deliberate eye roll. "You're unbelievable, do you know that?"

Hudson tried to make out that he didn't know what Liberty was referring to, but his slightly giddy grin gave him away.

Tory stepped purposefully forward until she reached the older woman and stocky man, who had turned to face her. Both were blocking her route to the bar. Tory could have gone around them, but Hudson knew that wasn't her style. It was then that Hudson noticed Tory's antique six-shooter was still in her holster, in open defiance of station regulations. He tensed up, realizing that one or both of the two people blocking Tory's path were about to make a terrible mistake.

"You're in my way," said Tory, looking first at the woman, then up into the eyes of the stocky man.

Mullet man was obviously still smarting from being beasted around by Liberty, and was in no mood to take shit from anyone else. "Who do you think you are?" he asked, and then he made another fateful mistake. He shoved Tory in the chest and added, "Why don't you piss off back out that door, sweetheart?"

Tory grabbed the man's wrist, twisted it so that his elbow was facing her, and then struck it with her forearm. It was every bit as slick and as fast as any of Liberty's moves, but delivered with ten

12

times the aggression. Hudson heard the tendons snap and ligaments rip from the bone as the elbow was broken. He'd never heard a sound quite so gut-wrenching in his life, until the man started screaming.

Tory then looked over at the woman, and raised her eyebrows by the slightest fraction. However, this was more than enough to convey her message clearly, assuming the sight of the man, cradling his broken elbow, hadn't already done the trick. The older woman raised her hands and backed away.

"Look, I don't want any trouble, Tory," the woman said, her voice wavering. Then she pointed towards the bar. "My quarrel was only with that no-good hustler over there."

Tory scowled and then looked over to the bar, locking eyes with Liberty. Then she noticed Hudson, and her clinical stare instantly relaxed. The huff and tut from Liberty indicated that she had noticed Tory's sudden change of demeanor too.

Tory Bellona continued her measured steps into the bar, while all eyes remained on her. She stopped briefly in front of them both, nodded at Liberty, drawing a baffled frown in response, then slid onto a stool next to Hudson. Her eyes remained fixed ahead, staring towards the back wall. After several excruciating, silent seconds had elapsed, she met Hudson's eyes and said, "Well, are you going to buy me a drink, or not?"

CHAPTER 2

Logan Griff rubbed his aching neck and temples as he waited impatiently outside the office of Superintendent Jane Wash. He'd stepped off his patrol craft less than an hour earlier, after an uncomfortable one-point-five-g transit from Earth, and felt utterly drained. He had not been informed of the reason why Wash had transferred him to RGF headquarters in Gale City on Mars, and was hacked off at the order. He hated Mars, its stuck-up inhabitants and the arrogant MP military even more than he hated portal world dwellers.

The newly-promoted Superintendent Wash had recently been assigned as the commander of RGF operations in the MP region. Since Griff had been Wash's chief source of under-the-table income while she was stationed in CET territory, he assumed this had something to do with his hasty summons. Griff had made Wash very rich already, and she no doubt intended that their arrangement should continue.

Wash opened the door and stood in the threshold, wearing her full-dress uniform. Griff's eyes slid over her body and then he shuddered, catching himself in the act. Even Griff had standards, or at least that's what he told himself.

Luckily, Wash hadn't spotted Griff checking her out, as she'd looked across to the opposite side of the corridor first. Griff was glad of this; he'd hate Wash to think she had any more power over him than she already did. Wash then spotted the lounging, lanky frame of Logan Griff, slumped back on the couch, and cleared her throat, obviously. "You can come in now, Corporal," she called over to him, before walking back to her desk and leaving the door open. Griff forced his aching muscles to lift his numb backside off the couch, and slouched into the office, leaving the door open behind him.

Wash tutted loudly, "Close the door, you idiot," she screeched, looking at Griff as if he was a vagrant that had just sauntered in off the street. She then sat down in her plush, red leather armchair, and gestured to a plain-looking guest chair that was already set out. "And then sit down."

Grudgingly, Griff shut the door and flopped into the chair before looking around the office. Like most Martian décor, it was clean and functional and, at least in Griff's opinion, deathly dull. The

Martians had refused to adopt Earth-based styles of design, preferring to create their own 'brand'. It reminded Griff of a modern Scandinavian style, but with polymers and metals instead of wood. This was because the few trees that existed inside the domed habitats of Mars were far too valuable to harvest. And the Martians, being the arrogant, self-important assholes that they were, refused to import anything from Earth. Wash's red leather chair was a rare and likely prohibited Earthly creature-comfort that spoke volumes about her general disregard for the rules.

"I said sit down, not slouch down," snapped Wash, clearly disturbed by Griff's disheveled appearance. "You look like a damn crack addict."

Griff groaned and straightened up. "No disrespect, ma'am, but why the hell have you dragged me out here?" he began, starting as he meant to go on. He and Wash shared a special relationship that meant the usual stuffy, rank-based formality had been dispensed with long ago. "You know I can't stand this red lump of crap."

"And you know I don't care," replied Wash, tersely. "I've transferred you here so that we can continue our mutually-beneficial arrangement."

Griff snorted a laugh, "I don't see how forcing me to cover that traitor Hudson Powell's quota is mutually beneficial," he replied, folding his arms.

Wash smiled, "Perhaps you'd prefer it if I let you fester in a CET cell on one of their delightfully austere prison stations?" She allowed Griff an opening to add another snide remark, but he knew better than to fall into her trap. "Or, I can very easily arrange a stay at one of the choicest penitentiaries in the Union of Outer Portal Worlds, if you like?"

Griff bit his tongue again, knowing that Wash was perfectly able to make good on such a threat. He hated always being on the back foot against his superior officer. Wash held all the cards, all the time. This included the important 'get out of jail free' card that she'd used to keep Griff out of lock-up in the past.

"You know I'm grateful for you squaring things so that I stay clean," Griff answered, reluctantly. "All I'm saying is that I'd be more motivated if I actually got to see some of the fruits of my labors. Everything I took from that asshole Powell on Bach Two just went into meeting my extended quota."

Wash seemed to consider this for a moment then got up out of the chair, stepping over to an infopanel on the side wall. "That's actually why I called you here," she said, tapping the infopanel twice, which turned the windows of her office opaque. "You were the first RGF officer on site at the newly discovered portal world, Zimmer One, correct?"

Griff frowned. "The portal world that Powell and his maniac partner found?" Wash nodded.

"Yeah, I was there, for all the good it did me. That pompous CET Commodore, Trent, denied me our take. And then he let Powell and the girl walk off with everything."

"Table scraps..." said Wash, practically spitting the words. "Your petty vendetta against that man is clouding your judgement, and making you think small." Then she activated the infopanel and brought up an image of a crystal. It was a little blurry, and looked to be a magnified part of a larger image. "Do you know what this is?" Wash asked. Then before Griff could retort with one of his characteristically acerbic comebacks, she added, "and don't say, 'it's a crystal'."

Griff hauled himself upright and ambled up to the infopanel. "I've never seen it before, though there were rumors of some alien crystal being found on the wreck at Brahms Three." Then Griff's eyes narrowed, as his addled brain began to connect the dots. "Thinking back, it was Ericka Reach – the hunter I wasted – who supposedly had it. But I searched her ship and the CET vault on the planet, and I never saw it."

"The CET vault that Hudson Powell locked you in, after getting the better of you?" said Wash, raising one of her razor-thin eyebrows. Then after a slight pause, she added, "Excuse me, I mean after he got the better of you, *again...*"

If it had been any other person, Griff would have hit back, probably with his fists. However, he knew that any such act would simply incur further penalties from his vindictive commander. Wash wasn't corrupt just so that she could get rich. She actually got a sadistic kick out of making other people miserable, and Griff wasn't going to give her the satisfaction.

"Yes, that's the one," answered Griff, trying to stay calm. "And, like I said, I didn't see any crystal." Then it was his turn to add a pause for effect, "And I had plenty of chance to look, before I busted *myself* out, without getting caught."

Wash smiled and tapped the infopanel again. The image zoomed out, showing a camera feed of a small store, with two men inside. One was behind the counter, and the other in front of it, with the crystal object on the counter top between them.

"I acquired these images of a hacked security feed from an antiques shop in the Bayview area of San Francisco," Wash went on. "Do you recognize either of these men?"

Griff assumed it was a loaded question, otherwise Wash wouldn't have asked. He did recognize the store owner, though it was someone he hadn't had dealings with for some time. "That guy is a prick called Cortland," said Griff, stabbing his finger onto the infopanel and leaving a greasy smear. "He's useful if you need to move stuff quickly, though I haven't seen him in years." Then Griff turned his attention to the other figure. "And unless you think I have intimate knowledge of the backs of people's heads, I'm not sure what you want me to say about the other guy."

"Look more closely, Corporal," snarled Wash. "You're supposed to be a damned investigator, after all."

Griff scowled at Wash, but she had goaded him, and he wanted to prove her wrong. He studied the image in more detail, and after a few seconds, he spotted that the customer's face had been reflected in a mirror behind the counter. Griff shook his head and sighed, "I should have guessed... Hudson Powell," he said, speaking the words through gritted teeth. "So, that's his trick. He somehow got this crystal from Ericka Reach and figured out what it does."

"I'd argue that his partner, Liberty Devan, likely did the figuring out," Wash cut in, "but yes. This crystal is the key that unlocks the new portals. I am sure of it."

"And whoever has the crystal has exclusive access to all the undiscovered alien wrecks," added Griff, now finally understanding why Wash had dragged him to Mars. "You want to claim the first-finder rights for the RGF?"

Wash shook her head, "Stop thinking small... No, I want much more than that," she said, in a darkly sinister way that made even Griff's thick skin crawl. "I'm sick of pandering to the CET, the MP and the OPW. I'm sick of just taking a small slice, in return for making them richer. It's time the RGF branched out."

"You want to claim these worlds for the RGF?" said Griff, smiling and showing his yellow teeth underneath his wiry black mustache. He didn't especially like Wash, but he admired her ruthlessness, and he couldn't deny that she had balls. Creating a separate RGF faction was a gutsy ambition, and one that would not only make her immensely rich, but throw the current economic system into disarray. However, like Wash, he didn't give a shit about the CET or any other controlling authority, so long as it lined his pockets too.

"You get me that crystal, and you won't just be taking a small slice of the profits," Wash continued, moving more quickly now that Griff seemed to be on-board. "I'll make you governor of one of the new planets we discover." Griff's eyes lit up as she said this. "One of the new RGF worlds. Our worlds. Then you can take a slice of everything. You'll live like a king; how does that sound, Corporal Griff?"

Griff rubbed his neck and peered back at the image of Hudson Powell in the antiques shop. This was the perfect way to get his revenge. He'd rob him of his famous discovery, ruin him and then kill him. However, Powell wouldn't die before Griff made sure that the asshole knew who it was that had gotten the better of him.

"I'll get you this alien crystal," Griff said, determinedly. "But I'll need to be released from regular duties. I'll need to be able to pursue this, wherever it leads, with broad authority."

Wash moved back to her desk and slid open a drawer in the anemic looking piece of polymer furniture. She removed an ID card and a shield badge and placed them on the desk in front of where Griff had been sitting. He moved over to the desk and picked up the ID card first. It read, 'Inspector Logan Griff, special investigations branch, Relic Guardian Force.' He smiled and picked up the shield, rubbing his nicotine-stained thumb lovingly over the metal. "What's the special investigations branch?" he asked, before looking up at Wash. "I've never heard of them before."

Wash smiled, "It's a department of one. You." Then she slammed the drawer shut, sat back down in her red leather chair and pointed to the door. "Now, go and get me that crystal, Inspector Griff."

Griff stood up and turned to leave, eager to test the limits of his new authority. However, before he'd reached the door, Wash then called out again.

"And, Inspector, don't let this petty squabble with the traitor, Powell, cloud your judgement," she said. "If you can get rid of him in the process then fine, but the crystal is what matters, not your pride. Are we clear?"

"Crystal clear, ma'am," said Griff, smiling at his own joke, before opening the door and stepping through. However, he had no intention of letting Powell off the hook, no matter what Wash said. The thought of his own planet and the riches that came with it was intoxicating, but so long as Powell still breathed, he'd never be content.

CHAPTER 3

Liberty had complained non-stop since they had both left The Winchester. Her primary grievance had been leveled at Hudson, for insisting she hand over some of her poker winnings to pay for the damages to the bar. Liberty's argument had been that she hadn't started the brawl in the first place, and so shouldn't be saddled with the cost of making reparations. However, Hudson's reasoned response had been along the lines of, 'it takes two (or in the case of that particular brawl, four) to tango'. In other words, she'd played her part. And besides, it was always helpful to stay on the good side of barkeeps in the more dangerous portal worlds and stations. He'd then cited Martina from the Landing Strip on Brahms Three as the prime example.

Her other complaint had been that she'd been forced to wait while Hudson and Tory Bellona enjoyed an intimate tête-à-tête over a glass of whiskey. Hudson couldn't easily begrudge her this grumble, especially since the two of them had exchanged very few words in the short time they'd spent together. Even so, it had felt like a breakthrough. He knew Tory was dangerous, and that she'd done things that would trouble him deeply, but he could feel in his bones that she wasn't a bad person. The problem was that Cutler Wendell had some kind of hold over her. Until he could find out what this was, and how he could break it, she would never be free to tread her own path.

"Come on, you must still have about four grand tucked inside that jacket," Hudson said, after Liberty had complained about paying for the bar damages for the third time. "I don't even know how you managed to fit it all in there."

"That's not the point, and you know it," said Liberty, still refusing to let it go.

Hudson kept quiet. He knew the true reason for her continued bad mood was that it had been Tory who'd casually broken up the fight. She'd made her dislike of the mercenary clear, and still regularly warned Hudson not to trust her.

"What did you two talk about, anyway?" Liberty added, as if she'd read Hudson's thoughts. "Over your cosy little drink, I mean."

"Nothing much," Hudson shrugged. "I asked her what brought her to Deimos, and she just said, 'work'."

Liberty laughed, "You realize that 'work' likely means helping Cutler to kill us, right?"

Hudson shushed her and continued, "And then I said something like, 'it's good to see you', and then we drank, and that was that."

"With small-talk like that, I can see why you're such a hit with the ladies..." replied Liberty.

"Don't be so hard on her," Hudson hit back. "I have a feeling about Tory, that's all. You of all people should be able to empathize with that. You took a chance on me, without knowing anything about who I was. Besides, I like that she's more a woman of action than words."

"I think the action you have in mind is different to the murderous thoughts that are rattling around her empty skull."

Hudson nudged Liberty, knocking her off balance, "Don't be so filthy." Then he stopped and looked around, "Where the hell are we, anyway? These Martian stations all look the same."

Liberty took the lead, shoulder-barging Hudson as she passed. "Our docking section is just up here on the left," she said, smiling back at him.

"What would I do without you, co-captain?" said Hudson, returning the smile.

"Well, for starters, you'd probably get lost," said Liberty, and then they both turned the corner, laughing. However, their amusement was short-lived, as standing in front of the Orion was the bald stocky man from the bar fight, flanked by two others. His companions shared the bald man's round face, stub nose, and thick-set frame, and all three were holding short metal bars. They looked like a trio of hired henchmen from a bad spy thriller movie.

"Your friend broke Dillard's elbow," the bald man said. "You owe me for that, and for the hardbucks you cheated out of me in the game."

"She's not our friend, and I don't owe you a damn thing," Liberty hit back. "So, unless you want me to kick your ass again, I suggest you 'scoot'." Liberty again did the little walking gesture with two fingers.

Hudson winced and took a step towards the trio, holding up his hands. If he'd had a white flag, he would have been waving it. Unlike Liberty, he was far less keen to get into another brawl, especially with three men who all looked like proverbial brick shithouses. "Look, guys, there's no need for violence, I'm sure we can come to some sort of arrangement." He couldn't see Liberty, but he was sure she was scowling at him at that moment, wondering if this 'arrangement' would involve her handing over more hardbucks.

The bald man aimed the metal pipe at Liberty, "She had the chance to make 'an arrangement' back in the bar," he spat. "So now I'm making demands instead. You're going to tell me and my brothers here how you detected that new portal. Or else we take a look inside your ship and find out for ourselves."

Hudson lowered his hands and rested his thumbs through his belt loops. "Guys, I'm trying to be reasonable, here, but honestly you're starting to piss me off." This wasn't just his 'tough guy' relic hunter persona talking; he was genuinely getting annoyed. "You're not getting on our ship. And because you've pissed me off, you're not getting anything else either. Besides, perhaps, another ass whooping."

The bald man sighed and shook his head. "Alright, if that's how you want to play this," he said, sounding almost glad that Hudson had given him the verbal middle finger. Then he casually handed his metal bar to one of his brothers behind him, and pulled a handgun out from behind his back.

Shit, he must have had it tucked into the back of his waistband, thought Hudson. Then he felt for his own pistol in the shoulder holster, before remembering that he'd left it on the ship, as per the station's rules.

"Not so cocky now, are we?" said the bald man, clicking off the safety on the handgun. Then he aimed the weapon at Liberty, causing Hudson's heart to leap in his chest. "Now, the Karate Kid over there is going to give me all of the hardbucks she cheated out of us." Hudson heard Liberty snort loudly in disgust. Though, he wasn't sure whether it was disgust at having to hand over the cash, or disgust at being accused of cheating, or both. Then the man aimed the weapon at Hudson, "And you, laughing boy, are going to show me how to find these undiscovered portals."

As tense situations went, this one ranked pretty highly. And given what Hudson had experienced over the last few weeks and months, that was saying something. He tried to think of a smart or even daringly stupid way out of the mess, but this time they were cornered. He glanced over to Liberty, and though she still gave off her usual defiant air, he could see that she was similarly at a loss for what to do.

"I'll give you until the count of three," the bald man said. "I don't have a problem with taking your ship's ID fob off your dead body, and searching the vessel myself."

Liberty stepped beside Hudson, seemingly in solidarity. "You're bluffing," she challenged him. "If you fire that in here, this hangar will be crawling with MP security before you can get within ten meters of our ship."

Hudson smiled – Liberty had a point. "She's right," he said, with matching tenacity, "you won't shoot."

"No, he won't."

Hudson and Liberty spun around to see Tory Bellona in the corridor outside the hangar. His eyes flashed back to the bald man, whose round face now looked as shocked as if someone had just whipped down his pants.

"But I will," Tory continued, before quick-drawing her antique Colt Frontier six-shooter, cocking it and firing in a single swift action that 'Wild Bill' Hickok would have been proud of. The shout of pain reached Hudson before he'd managed to turn to face the trio of brothers. This time, the bald man was on his back, cradling his shoulder, while being frantically attended to by the other men.

Hudson turned back to thank Tory, but she'd already gone. Instead, he looked at Liberty, who seemed just as astonished as he felt. Alarms then started to ring out inside the hangar and Hudson saw a squad of MP security guards rush inside, looking for the source of the commotion.

"Still think she's out to get us?" said Hudson, unable to withhold a grin.

"Yes," replied Liberty, without a moment's hesitation. "More than ever." Then she slapped him on the shoulder and they ran towards the Orion, eager to get out of sight before the security guards arrived. "Come on, I think we've outstayed our welcome."

CHAPTER 4

Logan Griff stubbed out his cigarette in the silver ash tray, which was the only item on the table, besides his steaming cup of black coffee. He then plucked a squashed cigarette packet from his shirt pocket, and slid out another smoke, while scanning his keen eyes around the room. The RGF officers' mess on Deimos Station was a small and generally depressing place. It conformed to the sort of bleak, minimalist Martian design that Griff hated. On the plus side, it was also quiet and off-grid, and perfect for the sort of clandestine meeting that Griff had planned. Besides the mess manager and two other officers in the far corner, it was also, importantly, private. And privacy was what Griff sought most of all at that moment.

Griff heard the door swing open and Cutler Wendell stepped inside, followed a second later by Tory Bellona. Griff's eyes immediately traced the curves of Tory's body, from the top of her chestnut hair to the tip of her reinforced boots, before he forced himself to look away. He'd witnessed first-hand how Tory handled people who stared at her the way he had just done. The urge to eyeball her again was still hard to resist, despite him knowing the likely consequences. Griff tapped the cigarette on the table, popped it into his mouth and lit it, while Cutler pulled up a chair and sat down. Tory also grabbed a chair, but instead of sitting down, she dragged it across the floor. It was a slow, deliberate action that generated a painful screeching sound, like a frightened pig. She then spun the chair around so that the back was facing the table and straddled it, all the while paying careful attention to where Griff was looking. Griff knew she was trying to goad him into gawping at her, to give her an excuse for a confrontation, but even so he nearly took the bait.

"Nice place," said Cutler, though because of his characteristically dry delivery, Griff couldn't tell if he was serious or being sarcastic.

Griff then saw the mess manager hurriedly approach the table. He walked up to Griff, but cast an anxious eye at Cutler and Tory too.

"This mess is for RGF officers only," the mess manager said, keeping his voice low and respectful. "I'm afraid that your guests will have to leave."

Griff blew out a thick plume of smoke, which Tory angrily wafted away, and then shifted sideways to look up at the mess manager. He casually removed his shield and ID from his belt and flopped the wallet open on the table.

"It's okay, they're on special investigations branch business," said Griff, though the mess manager's confused expression suggested that this meant nothing to him. The man bowed lower to read the ID, and then straightened up again. "Of course, Inspector Griff," he said, apologetically, though he still looked slightly bemused. Then he turned to Cutler and Tory and added, "May I get you anything?"

"Just a water," said Cutler, the tone of his voice as featureless as his expression.

"Whiskey," said Tory, and then she met the mess manager's nervous eyes. "And make it a large one." The mess manager nodded and hurried away.

"It seems that someone is going up in the world," said Cutler, tapping the shield on the table.

Griff smiled, showing the top row of his yellow teeth, and then reattached his ID and shield to his belt. "My good fortune is yours also," he said, as the mess manager returned, placing a tall glass of water on the table in front of Cutler. Then, with a less steady hand, he placed an obnoxiously large tumbler of whiskey in front of Tory, spilling some in the process.

"I'm so sorry," he said, quickly grabbing a cloth from his pocket to mop up the spillage.

Tory spun her chair around then picked up the glass, watching the man frantically dry the table. "If that had spilled onto me, you would have been," she said, before relaxing back in the chair and taking a sip of the liquor.

Griff let out a short chuckle as the mess manager quickly departed, and blew out another plume of smoke. "That's what I love about you, Tory," he said, sloping towards her and resting his hand, smoldering cigarette pressed between two fingers, next to his coffee cup. "Always direct, and to the point."

Tory placed her glass back on the table and then leaned in towards Griff. He froze, not wanting to recoil for fear of looking weak, but also not wanting to get jabbed in the mouth, either. However, instead of punching him, Tory then casually plucked the cigarette out of his hand. Griff scowled as she dropped it, lit end first, into his half-drunk cup of coffee, before reclining again and picking up her drink. She sipped it idly, looking bored.

"Why are we here, Griff?" asked Cutler, while Griff watched the cigarette stub float around in his coffee. "Hudson Powell and the girl are on this station right now. Every moment we delay here allows them time to escape."

Out of habit, Griff reached for his cigarette packet, but then caught Tory staring at him, like he was an ant she was about to stomp. He lowered his hand and pressed it together with his other on the table, before responding to Cutler. "There's been a slight change of plan," he began, careful to keep his attention focused on Cutler, given Tory's stormy mood. "Powell is in possession of an object that is of great interest to RGF command. You are to retrieve this object. All other considerations are secondary."

Cutler frowned, "What object?"

"It's a crystal. That's all you need to know."

The mention of a crystal seemed to stir Tory's interest. She was now watching Griff intently, hanging off his every word.

"I will need to know more than that, Inspector," Cutler replied, curtly. "I care more about seeing Hudson Powell dead than I do about retrieving some random object. If an act of mere petty thievery is what you're looking for then you've come to the wrong man."

Griff considered this for a moment, chancing a look at Tory, who was still absorbed in the discussion, before meeting Cutler's eyes again. "Okay, I'll tell you," he said, but then was quick to add, "but you have to swear on whatever code you mercenaries abide by to keep this between us."

Cutler nodded, his expression still flat and devoid of emotion.

Griff looked to Tory, "I need both of you to swear it."

"I speak for Tory also," Cutler cut in. "Her discretion and obedience are assured."

Tory's eyes flicked momentarily to Cutler, like a switchblade springing out of its handle. Her eyes narrowed a fraction, but then she returned her gaze to Griff. Her stare was so intense that Griff found himself needing to look away again.

"Fair enough, but what I tell you mustn't leave this room," Griff continued, lowering his voice to barely more than a whisper. Cutler nodded, and Griff continued, "RGF believes the crystal is the key to detecting undiscovered portals." For the first time since entering the officer's mess, Cutler's expression revealed a faint glimmer of interest. "If you retrieve this crystal intact, the RGF will compensate you one quarter of a percent of all taxes collected on any new worlds that it claims."

Cutler's eye's narrowed slightly, "On any new worlds that who claims?"

Griff sniffed, then wiped the corners of his mouth, while cautiously checking that no-one else in the mess was listening in. When he was satisfied they weren't being eavesdropped on, he leant in closer, again keeping his voice hushed and low. "The RGF intends to claim the new portal worlds under its own banner," said Griff, and this time Cutler's expression did give something away. He looked genuinely surprised. "That means all of the profits from the wrecks goes straight to the RGF, minus your cut, of course." Griff then rested back in the chair, feeling confident that he'd sold his proposition well. Even so, he wanted to make it as unambiguous as possible. "And I'm sure you don't need me to tell you that we're talking about a considerable sum of credits here. Maybe even billions..."

Cutler took a sip of his water, before glancing across to Tory. However, unlike Cutler, her expression had not altered during the entire exchange. If Tory had played poker, she would have been unreadable. Cutler then placed his glass down on the table, and nodded, "Then we are in agreement, Inspector Griff."

Griff smiled and then raised his coffee to his lips, before tasting ash and spitting the liquid back into the cup. Cutler's expression remained unchanged, but Tory's lips had curled into a serpentine smile. It seemed that talk of billions of credits wasn't enough to get a reaction from her, but seeing Griff make a fool of himself was. Griff placed the cup back on the table and angrily pushed it away. If it had been anyone other than Tory mocking him – even Cutler – he would have hit back. However, Tory was simply too unpredictable.

"So, what next?" asked Cutler, now appearing anxious to make a start on his new mission.

"We follow Hudson Powell and wait for him to uncover a new portal," Griff said, using the paper tissue that came with his coffee to dab ash from his tongue. "Then we follow him through. There will be a scramble for the wreck, with maybe a dozen hunters and a couple of RGF and MP ships. In the bustle and confusion, we will have an opportunity to grab Powell, and his pissant partner, and force them to tell us how the crystal works."

Cutler nodded again, but Griff could tell the question of Hudson Powell's fate had not slipped his mind. "And once we have this crystal, and an understanding of how it functions, I assume our original agreement stands?" asked Cutler.

"As soon as we have it, Powell is yours," replied Griff without delay. "But I want that piece of shit to know it was us that took him down."

"Dead is dead, Inspector," said Cutler. "But Hudson Powell has become a personal matter. You can be assured he will suffer."

Tory drank the remainder of her whiskey like it was water, and then pushed her chair back and stood up. "I'll get the ship ready for launch," she said to Cutler. Then without waiting for a response, she turned to Griff, and smiled. "Enjoy the rest of your coffee, Inspector..."

Griff watched as Tory walked away, this time free to check her out without fear of reprisal. Once she had gone, Griff turned back to Cutler. "Are you sure you can trust her?" he asked. As much as he enjoyed looking at Tory's ass, she was a closed book to him, and that made him nervous.

"I question many things about Tory Bellona, but not her loyalty," Cutler replied, taking another sip of his water.

"What is it with you two, anyway?" Griff went on, feeling emboldened to dig deeper, now the intimidating presence of Tory was absent. However, Cutler appeared unwilling to engage in a conversation about his menacing partner. "Come on, Cutler," Griff pressed, "I trusted you with a whole lot of confidential shit just now, so you can repay in kind."

Cutler pushed his chair back and stood up; his monochrome expression had returned. Then, to Griff's surprise, he actually answered the question. "I freed her."

Griff's eyes widened, "She was indentured?"

Cutler nodded, "She was sold to the owner of a corporation in the Outer Portal Worlds when she was nine. Soon, her talents drew the attention of the Council, which is where I ran into her, many years ago."

Griff blew out a long low whistle. The Council was the largest crime syndicate in the Outer Portal Worlds. If Tory had been indentured into their service, it explained a lot about her proficiency for violence, as well as her constant foul temper. And it also made Griff even more glad that she'd not caught him gawking at her.

Griff had personally spent very little time in the OPW territories. Despite the many opportunities that these more lawless worlds presented to a man like Griff, the risks were also far greater. However, he knew how certain organizations would indenture people, often children, into what was essentially a life of servitude. These indenturees would perform a variety of roles, almost none of which were legal. They were never permitted to leave, and were often fitted with explosive or toxic implants to ensure obedience. It was a profitable business, assuming you didn't get caught. A business, he realized, that his new status might open up to him. As an RGF Inspector, especially one from the ambiguous 'special investigations branch', he would be able to move freely inside the facilities these criminal organizations operated in, with a prisoner in tow. A prisoner that he could then sell to the Council for a hefty profit. The spark of an idea germinated in his mind, but he parked it for the time being. Griff wanted to get as much information out of Cutler as he could, while he was still in a compliant mood.

"How did you get her out?" asked Griff. Few people ever escaped a life of indentured service, especially to the Council. And especially when the individual's talents were so perfectly suited to the Council's often savage methods.

"The cost was high, in credits and in lives," answered Cutler, before turning to leave. Then he paused and glanced at Griff one last time. "But she has proven to be worth every penny. She will do whatever is required, of that you can be assured."

Cutler left and Griff called over the mess manager to settle the bill. While he was waiting, his eyes fell on Tory's whiskey glass, and he reached over to pick it up. He could see her lip mark on the rim of the glass, and then pictured the curve of Tory's mouth in his mind.

"Will that be everything, sir?" asked the mess manager, startling Griff by his sudden appearance.

"Yes, that's everything." Griff replied, lazily pressing his thumb to the credit scanner. He then lifted Tory's glass to his mouth, tipping the dregs of the whiskey onto his tongue, before licking his lips, and leaving.

CHAPTER 5

A friendly-sounding chirrup emanated from the navigation scanner, notifying Hudson that another ship had closed to within a kilometer of the Orion. He glanced down and saw that the total count was now fourteen. This included, inevitably, Cutler Wendell and Tory Bellona, plus two RGF Patrol Crafts and an MP Cruiser. While he didn't expect any protection from the RGF, Hudson actually felt relieved to see the powerful MP Cruiser on the scanner. He doubted even Cutler Wendell would be brazen enough to attempt anything with such a formidable military vessel close by. Hudson knew that Martians may have been stuck up, but they were also – for the most part – sticklers for rules and laws.

"It seems that we've gathered quite a following," said Hudson, glancing over to Liberty. "It's almost as if they're expecting something big to happen..."

Liberty smiled, "Well, pretty soon they might get their wish," she replied, while fine-tuning the settings on the scendar device.

The scendar, or Shaak Crystal Energy Detection And Ranging device, was a home-made contraption of Liberty's that was able to locate new portals. It used the alien crystal to detect the unique Shaak radiation signatures of the undiscovered gateways, and then open them, like a key. To their surprise, they had discovered that the nearest purple blip, indicating a new portal, had turned out to be next to Phobos, the sister moon to Deimos. This was a relatively short journey from Deimos Station, certainly compared to the fifty million kilometers they'd had to travel from Brahms Three to uncover the last portal. And it accounted for the relatively large cohort of eager hunters, all looking to plunder the potentially untouched alien wreck that everyone expected to find on the other side of the portal.

Liberty relayed the updated co-ordinates to Hudson, and then relaxed back in her seat. "I've just sent you a minor course correction, but we're almost on top of it now," she added, watching as the purple blip on the scanner crept ever closer.

"Got it," said Hudson, altering his heading to the new coordinates. All of the ships to their rear soon followed suit, as if they were tethered to the Orion via long tow-ropes. "Once we light up this portal, there's going to be a crazy rush to follow us through, so strap yourself in tight."

"I'm more worried about the chaos on the other side," said Liberty, ominously. "Fourteen ships, including that beast of a cruiser, all suddenly losing main drive... It will be like a day at the dodgems."

"Shit, I hadn't thought of that," admitted Hudson, as he pulsed the thrusters to kill their forward momentum. "We're going to need your tech genius to restart our engines again in double-quick time."

Liberty nodded and unclipped her harness. "I'll transfer to engineering, so I'm in place and ready as soon as we transit."

"You'll miss the pretty light show..." said Hudson, but Liberty just shrugged.

"Meh, you've seen one mysterious alien portal opening, you've seen 'em all." Then she stepped beside Hudson's seat and pointed to a program that was set up to run on the scendar. "Just hit that button when I'm in position and give you the signal. The scendar will then scan for the portal's resonant frequency and transmit the pulse. After that, we run like hell..."

"You don't need to tell me twice," replied Hudson, before placing his hand on the thruster lever and letting out a long breath. "I feel like we're a worm, surrounded by hungry crows."

Liberty jabbed him on the arm, "Hey, the Orion is an eagle not a worm," she said, and then headed for the exit. She hung back at the threshold and added, "So, get ready to soar."

Hudson threw up a casual salute as Liberty headed out of the cockpit. His eyes flicked to the navigation scanner again, noting that the fourteen other ships had begun to huddle around the Orion. Then the cockpit went dark, and Hudson looked up through the glass to see the imposing form of the MP Cruiser. It was so large that it had cast the Orion into shadow, though even this powerful military vessel was pint-sized compared to the alien hulks. Proximity alerts began to sound on his panel, and Hudson started to feel his pulse climb. The other ships were jostling for position, like soccer players awaiting a corner kick.

Come on, Liberty, any time now would be nice... Hudson urged, starting to feel like a sardine in the center of the tin. Then there was a sudden flash of light that lit up the cockpit and forced Hudson to shield his eyes. He looked left and saw that two relic hunter vessels had collided, and that one of them was on fire. "Shit!" he said out loud, and flipped open a communications channel to the engineering deck. "Whenever you're ready, Liberty," he called into his headset mic, "or there will be nothing left out here but burning debris."

"Give me ten seconds," came the crackly reply.

Hudson looked up again to see the flaming relic hunter ship slowly drifting towards him. A collision alert sounded and his grip on the controls tightened further. "Any more than ten seconds, and we won't be here..." he answered, trying to remain calm, but his voice had already climbed half an octave.

"Okay, run the scendar program, *now!*" Liberty called out.

Hudson hit the button on the panel so hard that he almost punctured it with his forefinger. The scendar device, fixed into a bay below the flight deck systems, then began to glow. Liberty's program started to rapidly cycle through Shaak radiation frequencies, until it found the resonant frequency of the portal. Hudson's eyes widened as the burning ship drifted closer, but he couldn't move without giving up his lead spot to another relic hunter. He had to hold his position, and his nerve.

Come on, open already! urged Hudson, as a reverberant thrum started to pulse through the deck plating. Then, as with the first time they'd activated a dormant portal, the lights dimmed as power was sucked from the ship's reactor and diverted into the crystal, causing it to glow like a lightbulb. Then there was a vivid purple flash of light.

"Hang on, I'm going in!" Hudson cried out into the microphone. The collision warning alarm rose to a shriek. Hudson pushed the throttle fully forward, accelerating the ship away from the burning mass, and into the new portal. There was another bright purple flash as the Orion passed the threshold, followed by a swirling pattern of dancing light and energy. Then within a matter of seconds, he was back in deep space again.

"Liberty, we're through!" Hudson called out again, "The race is on, so we need those engines..."

"Whatever you say, skipper" came the surprisingly calm reply, and then the channel clicked off.

Hudson tested the thrusters, which were still working, and pulsed the Orion away from the portal mouth. Suddenly there came a succession of bright purple flashes, as the first of the pursuing ships made the portal transition. Collision warnings again screeched out in the cockpit, as vessel after vessel appeared on the navigation scanner, some as close as twenty meters away.

"This is worse than being shot at!" Hudson called out, as he pushed the thrusters harder in order to steer the ship away from the emerging dangers. Then there was a brighter flash and the MP Cruiser emerged from the portal, directly into the midst of the throng of relic hunters. Its main drive engines blinked and then flashed out unevenly, kicking out the aft section like a shark's tail. It collided with a relic hunter freighter, crushing it's forward section like an egg. The energy of the impact propelled the stricken vessel towards a second hunter, like a baseball struck by a bat. With only thrusters to fall back on, the unfortunate courier runner was unable to evade the speeding projectile, and was hit head on. Seconds later, both ships exploded in a fiery blaze, sending burning debris in all directions. Hudson reacted on pure instinct, turning the Orion on its axis and pushing it away from one of the burning projectiles. There were dull thuds and scrapes as the metal skimmed off the Orion's hull, but the damage warning lights all stayed clear.

"What the hell was that?!" came the voice of a far less calm Liberty Devan over the communication channel.

"It's raining ships out here, so whatever you're doing, do it more quickly..." Hudson replied, making another adjustment to avoid a second hunk of debris.

Suddenly, the turret cannons on the MP Cruiser sprang into action, firing shells at the remaining fragments in a desperate attempt to destroy them. However, it was unable to prevent one of the larger hulks of metal from impacting a mid-sized shuttle. Compared to the bigger relic hunter freighters, this smaller ship didn't stand a chance. Its hull was smashed open, and its two occupants were blown out into space.

Liberty darted back into the cockpit and practically threw herself into her seat. "What the hell is going on out there?" she said, before spotting the burning ships.

"It's like the fourth of July, except the fireworks are relic hunters," replied Hudson. "Did you get the engines sorted?"

Liberty nodded, "They'll cycle back online in about a minute. Do we have a destination yet?"

With all the commotion, Hudson hadn't even checked the scans of the new system. He pulsed the thrusters to face the nearest planet, while still keeping a careful eye out for more debris. "There it is, though I can't tell you anything about it."

Liberty was already busy reading the scan results. "It's habitable, like all the other portal worlds. About fifty percent of the surface is covered in oceans, though it's a pretty barren-looking place overall."

Hudson's console chimed while Liberty was giving her analysis. He checked it, noting that there was a build-up of energy readings nearby. "Looks like some of the other ships out there are getting pretty adept at drive system re-starts too," he called over to Liberty. "We may not get as much of a head start as we thought." As soon as Hudson finished the sentence, the Orion's twin engines whirred back into life. He tested the engine pods and they responded. "We have power, I'm setting a course for the planet now."

"Wait..." Liberty called out, and Hudson's hand froze on the main throttle lever. "I'm detecting Shaak radiation from the planet, consistent with a wreck, though at curiously lower levels, but there's a second signature too."

Hudson frowned, "A second Shaak radiation signature? You mean there are two wrecks in this system?"

There was a momentary pause while Liberty continued to work at her console, before she clarified, "No, not a second ship." She threw up an image, overlaid on the cockpit glass in front of them. Liberty then looked at Hudson and the sparkle in her eyes was almost electric. "It's a space station."

Hudson's eyebrows hit his hairline, "An alien space station?" Liberty nodded. Then Hudson's console bleeped again. "Some of the other ships are powering up, so we need to make a call right now – planet or space station?"

Liberty smiled, "Why are you even asking? Space station of course!"

"Always the adventurer!" Hudson chuckled, and then he tightened the straps of his seat. "Get ready for a high-g burst; we're about to become the first humans to set foot on an alien space station!" Then he angled the nose of the Orion towards the second Shaak signature, and slammed the throttle fully forward.

CHAPTER 6

Liberty's rapid drive systems restart had given the Orion an advantage in the race towards the new alien station, but not by much. They had gained a couple of minutes at most, before the first wave of relic hunters caught up with them.

Only ten ships had survived the transit through the portal, besides the Orion, and this included the MP Cruiser and two RGF Patrol Craft. That left eight other relic hunters, with Cutler Wendell's FS-31 amongst them.

"Looks like five are heading for the planet and the other three are angling for the station, like us," said Liberty.

"Let me guess, Cutler is one of the ones heading to the station, right?" said Hudson, with a raise of his right eyebrow.

"No, he's heading to the planet."

Hudson jerked his head to face her, "Really?" However, Liberty's sardonic smile told him she was just pulling his leg. "Damn it, Liberty, you had me going for a moment then."

"Sorry..." said Liberty, in a way that suggested she wasn't really sorry. "Though, I'm actually beginning to think the planet is a better option."

"That sounds ominous," replied Hudson, starting to decelerate hard so they could approach the alien station at a more maneuverable speed.

"For some reason, I didn't even consider basics, like gravity and atmosphere," Liberty went on. "As in, the planet has them, and the station doesn't."

Hudson rubbed his eyes. He hadn't considered that either, and felt stupid for not doing so. He'd just heard the words, 'space station', and assumed it would be as simple as docking at Deimos. "Right, that might be a problem."

"Shall we alter course to the planet, instead?" asked Liberty, "We've lost our lead, but there's still plenty to go around, before the MP or RGF have a chance to call time on the initial hunts."

Hudson nodded, "Okay, but let's fly past the station en-route. Who knows, there might be some pockets that still have pressure, or maybe we'll spot something valuable that we can scoop into the hold."

Liberty agreed and they continued on course, but it wasn't long before they realized it was no ordinary space station. "That thing is massive," she said reading the more detailed scans. "It's practically a small moon, almost half the size of Deimos." Then she seemed to become distracted as additional information flashed onto her screen. "Hold up, there seems to be a ship docked there."

Hudson's eyebrows hit his hairline again. "Docked at the station? Send me the co-ordinates, and I'll swing past it."

Liberty relayed the position, but she was frowning now. "No, I was wrong; it's not docked, but impaled into the station. From the looks of it, it's the same design as the alien wrecks on the portal worlds. But it's like the thing has been split in half through the mid-section."

"What the hell sort of weapon could do that?" wondered Hudson, feeling the hairs on the back of his neck tingle. The Orion passed around the far side of the station, and then Hudson saw what Liberty's scanners had detected first. He could scarcely believe what he was seeing. There was half of an alien wreck smashed into the side of the space station, protruding like the spout of a teapot.

Suddenly the lights in the cockpit dimmed, and the crystal in the scendar device began to glow. "Hey, Liberty, tell me you know why it's doing that," said Hudson, feeling his stomach tighten into a knot. At the back of his mind, he was still worried that Liberty's home-made contraption might explode, irradiate them or otherwise take them out in some other grisly manner.

"I'd love to," said Liberty, who was now frantically paging through different screens of information, across multiple monitors. "Shit, I forgot to shut the scendar down after activating the portal. It has been cycling through Shaak radiation frequencies for all this time."

"Are you saying it's found another portal?" asked Hudson.

Liberty shook her head, "Not another portal. More like another alien power source. Wait... something's happening."

Hudson was about to yell back, 'What?! What's happening?!', but the answer had already become apparent. Directly outside the cockpit, they could now see the space station coming to life. Lights flickered on all across its vast surface, and the indicator on Hudson's Shaak radiation scanner went through the roof.

"Did we..." Hudson paused, realizing the question he was about to ask sounded ridiculous, but he asked it anyway. "Did we just turn that alien space station on?"

Liberty's expression was again almost giddy with excitement. "I think so!" Then she quickly assimilated the new readings and added, "And it appears to be rapidly pressurizing, or at least sections of it that are not damaged are. It's an Oxygen-Nitrogen atmosphere, just like the planet. I'm detecting a gravity field too."

"Oxygen-Nitrogen, just like Earth..." Hudson added, though he was more thinking out loud. The fact they kept stumbling upon worlds that were hospitable to human life was improbable enough. However, that they'd now discovered a city-sized space station with breathable air was almost a step too far into an absurd new reality. Even more puzzling was where all the inhabitants had gone.

"If our shape-shifting alien, Morphus, ever does show up again, remind me to ask him what happened to the damn people," said Hudson.

Liberty visibly shuddered, as if someone had stepped on her grave. "Honestly, I'm not sure I want to know..." she answered.

Hudson then noticed his communications panel light up, and he huffed a laugh. "We're receiving a message from the MP Cruiser," he said, checking the text-only communication. "It was sent to all ships. Message reads, 'All relic hunter vessels, immediately cease scavenger operations and return via portal to MP space. Unknown alien anomaly detected in system. Military jurisdiction is established'."

Liberty scowled back at Hudson, "Really? Can they do that?"

"Honestly, I have no idea," replied Hudson, "but I don't see any of the other ships obeying that command."

"If we leave now, we get nothing," said Liberty. "By the time they let us back, the MP and RGF will have already established their cordons, and taken the juiciest relics for themselves."

Hudson sighed and grabbed the controls, before pushing the thruster lever forward.

Liberty half-frowned, half-smiled, "What are you doing?"

Hudson pointed out through the glass to a section of the space station. "That looks like a nice place to dock," he said, aiming his finger at what looked like an open bay area. "We lock on to the station's hull, cut through, and do what we came here to do."

Liberty laughed, "So rebellious, I love it!"

The navigation scanner bleeped and Hudson checked it quickly, before letting out another sigh. "Don't get too excited yet," he said, in a darker tone. "Three other hunters are following us into the space station, and one of them is..."

Liberty cut Hudson off, before he finished the sentence. "Don't tell me, FS-31 Patrol Craft Hawk-1333F. Cutler Wendell and Tory Bellona..."

CHAPTER 7

Hudson piloted the Orion deeper inside the cavernous interior of the alien station, sweeping the searchlight across the inner walls. Though it was unmistakably unearthly in design, to Hudson's eyes, it certainly had the appearance of a docking area. There were organized sectors, with what looked like docking hatches, plus platforms and docking arms that weren't hugely dissimilar to human designs. However, despite all the evidence pointing to its use as a docking bay, there was one crucial element missing – there were no ships.

"This place is giving me the creeps," said Hudson, as he continued to make his sweep inside. "This bay is large enough to accommodate hundreds of ships, but it's as dead as a ghost town."

"Well, there's more than one ship in it now," commented Liberty. "The other three hunters are also snooping around inside. We've even been joined by one of the RGF patrol craft."

Hudson scrunched up his nose. "RGF, why would they be in here? Their role is to set up the initial checkpoint perimeter and Shaak scanners."

"Beats me," replied Liberty, "but they're the least of our worries. Cutler's in here too."

"Oh, don't worry, I've got that shady bastard marked in red on my navigation scanner," said Hudson. "If he strays too close, then we introduce him to our new nose cannon."

Hudson had expected Liberty to give her enthusiastic endorsement of this suggestion, but instead she just raised her eyebrows and gave a noncommittal nod. "You don't agree with blowing Cutler to atoms?" asked Hudson. "Are you feeling okay?"

"Oh, I agree," said Liberty. "If I'm honest, I think giving them both barrels right now is one hundred percent our best option."

"But..." prompted Hudson.

Liberty smiled, "But when it comes down to it, I don't think you'd fire on that ship, knowing that Tory was inside. Admit it..."

Hudson had gotten used to Liberty's little jibes about Tory, and if he was honest, he had no desire to harm his mercenary guardian angel. Even so, if it came down to protecting them and the Orion, he wouldn't hesitate, and he needed Liberty to know that.

"Hey, don't think for one second I won't put that ship down if it threatens us," said Hudson, fixing Liberty with a cold stare. "I admit that I may have a bit of a thing for Tory..."

"A *bit*?" Liberty interrupted, with another raise of her eyebrows.

"Okay, maybe I like her more than a bit," Hudson yielded, "but I like what we have here a whole lot better."

Liberty nodded respectfully, acknowledging the sincerity of Hudson's words. Then she too became more serious. "And if it came down to it, and you could only save one of us from dying a cold, lonely death on this station. Who would you choose?"

"Come on, Liberty, what the hell kind of question is that?" said Hudson. He was genuinely offended.

"It's a question I need you to answer," Liberty replied, unmoved by Hudson's affronted reaction. "And I need you to look me in the eyes when you say it."

Hudson turned his seat fully to face Liberty and locked eyes with her. "It should go without saying," he began, almost angry at being forced to put it into words. "But since you need to hear it, then listen well. There is no choice. No question. No doubt. In a toss-up between you and *anyone* else, it will always be you. You got that?"

Liberty returned a shaky smile, but then turned away, so that Hudson couldn't see her face. He was about to say more, when he saw sparks flying into space from one of the other relic hunter ships. It had already locked on to the station's outer wall and was cutting through. He checked Cutler's position then adjusted the nose of the Orion so he could get a visual. Cutler's FS-31 was also thrusting up to the bay wall in an effort to hard-dock.

"Come on, the other ships are cutting through," said Hudson, pushing the Orion up to the nearest docking port – or at least the nearest thing that he assumed was a docking port. "We have some relic hunting to do, assuming you're still game for adventure?"

Liberty cleared her throat and then turned back to face Hudson, looking energized and fearless. "Last one on-board buys the drinks when we land back at Deimos."

"Well, since you still have all the hard bucks stuffed inside your jacket, that doesn't seem like much of a threat," said Hudson, "But I'll race you anyway."

Hudson attached the Orion onto the wall of the space station, then they ran through the ship to the auxiliary docking ring. Together they worked fast, using cutting torches to penetrate the seals surrounding the alien docking hatch. He'd left plenty of space between them and the other hunters, who had all docked in a similar manner. This included the RGF Patrol Craft, which Hudson again found unusual. From his RGF academy training days, he didn't recall there ever being a procedure for an occurrence such as this. Still, docking at the station seemed like an unnecessary move, when the RGF's main role was to establish a checkpoint perimeter. He'd conveyed his concern to Liberty, but she was too caught up in the moment to be interested.

"Masks on, until we can check out the air quality inside," said Hudson, as he began to melt through the final seal of the docking hatch. Liberty nodded, and together they pulled their respirators over their mouths and noses. Hudson cut through the final seal, deactivated his torch and stepped away. Seconds later Liberty did the same, and the door fell inwards with a weighty thud as it hit the inner deck. A rush of cold air blew in to the Orion's docking section, like an arctic wind.

"Shit, this place is freezing!" complained Hudson, rubbing the tops of his arms. His voice sounded oddly robotic and menacing through the respirator mask. "I need to add some arctic wear options to our relic hunter liveries."

Liberty practically jumped through the hatch and then turned to face Hudson. "You also need to buy the next round on Deimos," she said, before doing a sort of celebratory shuffle. "I set foot inside first!"

Hudson shook his head and stepped through after her. "What you actually need to do is stop dancing around, and test the air to see if it's breathable." Then he reached back inside the Orion and secured the inner docking door. "The Orion's all locked up; the last thing we need is some asshole hunter stealing our ship."

"Good thinking," said Liberty, who was now walking around the new room, while looking at a wristpad attached to her left arm. "The air seems clean. A tad oxygen-heavy, but nothing that will cause us any problems."

Hudson joined her and then surveyed their new location. It was a rectangular room, with exposed pipework and a generally industrial-looking vibe. However, it also looked like it had been the site of a major skirmish, sometime in the distant past. There were scorch marks, craters in the deck and walls, and rubble littered all around them. Hudson pulled off his respirator and hooked it to the side of his rucksack. The air was still cold, but there was no odor that Hudson could detect. It was no different to standing in an air-conditioned room on Deimos or any other station, except that it was maybe ten degrees colder.

"Looks like there was a fight on this station," said Hudson, inspecting some of the marks. "But between who, I shudder to think."

Liberty also removed her respirator, and then examined some of the damage. "I think I'd rather not find out. These are some pretty serious blast marks." Then she focused her attention on some of the other damage, running her hand across what looked like slash marks. "Explosive damage I can understand, but I wonder what made these gashes in the deck."

Hudson also inspected one of the cuts, and then noticed that there were all over, not just on the deck, but on the walls too. He shook his head and stood up, feeling even colder than the air around him. "I think this is another one of those things to file under, 'I'd rather not know'."

Liberty stepped away from the wall and checked for exits, spotting three corridors leading away from the room. "Come on, let's see what we can score. I don't want to hang around here longer than we have to, especially with the other hunters running around."

Hudson nodded and then drew the pistol from the shoulder holster inside his leather jacket. Liberty scowled at the weapon. "Hey, better safe than sorry," said Hudson, remembering Liberty's dislike of firearms. "I doubt these other hunters you mention will be happy to share. Anything goes in here, so we need to be ready."

Liberty grudgingly agreed and then together they moved off, picking a corridor at random. Hudson scouted ahead, while Liberty dug around inside panels that had been damaged or blown open, occasionally returning to drop items into Hudson's rucksack. They continued on in this way, until they reached a large double door, big enough that they could have driven a taxi flyer through it.

It was partially open in the center, and Hudson pressed his face to the crack and peered inside.

"Looks like this could perhaps be some sort of storage bay," said Hudson, seeing stacks of containers and what looked like racks and lockers.

Liberty yanked off a panel to the side of the door and peered at the circuitry inside. "Maybe I can hotwire it, and get it open," she said, pulling a couple of tools from a pouch on her belt.

Hudson stepped back and frowned. "Do you have any idea how this stuff works? This is, in case you've forgotten, an alien space station."

Liberty smiled at him. "I don't have the faintest idea how it works," she said, while poking one of her tools inside the panel. "But assuming it's an electrical circuit of some kind, how different can it really be?"

Hudson took another step back from the door. "I again feel the need to remind you about not blowing us both to hell..."

"That's rich coming from the guy who stuck a hand into some alien goop and accidently activated a shape-shifting artificial intelligence..."

Hudson scowled, but once again Liberty had a point, and he had no come back.

Just then there was a spark from the panel and a puff of smoke. A second later the giant double-doors whirred open. Liberty pulled her head out from the panel and beamed at Hudson. Her cheeks were covered in a light dusting of a black, soot-like substance, and her expression was smugness personified.

"Am I good or what?" she said, adding a slight bow and a flourish.

Hudson was about to congratulate her, when a tremor rumbled through the deck, like a low-level Earthquake. Liberty immediately lost her swagger.

"I'm sure that wasn't me..." Liberty hastily added, holding up her hands. "Or, well, I'm sort of sure, anyway."

Hudson wasn't convinced, and as he shot an anxious glance back at Liberty, she looked as guilty as a puppy sitting next to a chewed-up slipper.

CHAPTER 8

Logan Griff edged along the corridor of the space station, his weapon held ready. He was careful to stay hidden from the other relic hunter crews that were racing ahead, deeper inside the alien outpost. However, unlike the hunters, his goal wasn't to find new alien relics. His target was something that had already been discovered.

Griff raised his wristpad, scrolled to the name he wanted, and hit the 'call connect' button. A few seconds later, Cutler Wendell answered. "I'm on-board, and heading towards Powell's ship now," said Griff, flattening his body to the wall as a trio of hunters ran along an intersecting corridor.

"Understood, we'll meet you there," replied Cutler in his trademark, droning tenor. Griff could hear the sound of boots thumping against metal in the background. "I'd estimate that we'll arrive in five minutes. Wendell, out."

The channel went dead, and Griff lowered his wrist, scowling. "I might be shot dead by one of these low-life relic hunters in five minutes..." he grumbled. Then he continued towards where Hudson Powell's ship was locked-on to the outer wall. He checked ahead, but the sound of boots clomping on the alien deck had gone. The coast was clear. "To hell with them; I'm not waiting," he muttered under his breath, before stepping over the cut-out hatch lying on the deck and in to the docking ring of the Orion.

Griff pulled on the door release lever, but it was locked. He laughed. *Maybe you're not quite as dumb as you used to be, rook...* he thought. He'd half-expected Hudson to have left his ship wide open. Griff stole another look outside to satisfy himself that no-one was sneaking up on him, then pried open a panel underneath the door release controls. He then attached a cable from his wristpad to the exposed service port on the Orion's docking hatch, and initiated a bypass.

Over many years, the RGF had developed a sort of electronic skeleton key. The technology had been stolen and sold to the Council sometime later. It was this that had formed the basis of the 'skellies' that the more disreputable hunters and mercenaries used to break into places they shouldn't be. In a similar way, Griff's legitimate RGF device was designed to hack standard ship locking systems and allow officers access to abandoned relic hunter vessels. These ships, left over after their unfortunate owners died due to misadventure – or murder – inside a wreck, were considered 'spoils of war'. However, while the program's use outside of this official purpose was highly illegal, Griff's unique new position afforded him certain special privileges.

The distant sound of gunfire forced Griff to arch his long, thin neck to look behind. He'd spent only a few minutes on the station, but already he was itching to get back to his own ship. He hated the wrecks and alien technology in general, but that the space station was active made it ten times worse. It was like standing in a cemetery where the dead rose around you, instead of remaining quietly entombed in their graves.

The wristpad bleeped and then the hatch lock flashed green. "Finally," Griff muttered, yanking the door open.

"Bang!" a voice shouted out behind him.

Griff wheeled around, panic rising in his gut, and fumbled for his sidearm. Yanking it out of his holster, he then saw Tory Bellona standing in front of him, aiming her revolver at his head. Cutler was at her side.

"You're dead," Tory continued, before lowering the weapon.

"Shit, Tory, that wasn't funny!" roared Griff, noting that the revolver had actually been cocked. He let his arms fall to his sides and pressed his head back against the Orion's outer hull for support. "I could have shot you."

Tory casually decocked the antique weapon and holstered it. "You would have had to hear me coming to shoot me," she said, calmly. She was clearly gleaning some sadistic pleasure from tormenting him. "But you didn't."

"Can we just get on with this?" said Cutler, pushing past Tory and moving inside the Orion.

Tory raised her eyebrows and gestured to the open hatch. "After you, Inspector."

Griff holstered his weapon, then pushed away from the hull, before stepping inside the ship. Tory followed close behind, hand still resting on her six-shooter.

Despite the fright Tory had given him, Griff actually felt more relaxed now that the mercenary was there. However, his nerves were still frayed, like the end of an old, worn rope. He reached into his shirt pocket and pulled out a squashed packet of cigarettes in a plain black wrapper. Plucking out one of the sticks into his mouth using only his lips, he then returned the packet to his shirt, before lighting the stick and inhaling deeply. The hit took some of the edge off his fractious nerves, but he could sense Tory behind him, as if she was still pointing a gun to his head.

"Those things will kill you," complained Tory, before she added, with extra zeal, "hopefully..."

Griff laughed and blew out a plume of smoke above his head. "Not me, I'm a survivor," he hit back, sucking in another drag of the cigarette.

"You won't survive the next five minutes if you keep blowing that shit in my direction," Tory snarled.

Griff stopped and then waved Tory on, smiling at her with his yellow teeth. Tory brushed past him, waving her hands furiously in front of her face to clear the smoke, as if she was trying to swat a fly.

"VCX-110 Light Courier Runner," Cutler said out loud, while making his way on-board, "What a piece of junk."

"I like it," Tory said, as she moved past Cutler. Even with Cutler's hard-to-read facial expressions, Griff could see that her response had surprised the mercenary. "It's trustworthy and reliable. An honest ship," Tory went on, pressing the palm of her hand to the wall of the corridor.

Griff scowled and then blew another plume of smoke above his head. "I don't give a shit if it's the USS Enterprise, let's just find this crystal and get the hell off this station."

"I'll check the cockpit and main living space," said Cutler. "You two work aft. Check their living quarters, in case they've hidden it while they're both off the ship, and then move on to engineering."

"Hey, don't forget I give the orders around here," Griff said, jabbing his cigarette in Cutler's direction.

Cutler scowled, "Then what would like us to do, Inspector?"

Griff shrugged, "You go to the cockpit, and we'll work aft," he said, smiling.

"A brilliant plan," replied Cutler, dully, before moving towards the living space.

"Looks like you're with me," said Griff, indicating for Tory to go ahead.

"Lucky me," Tory answered, again wafting her hand to clear the smoke, and then marching off ahead.

Griff and Tory then worked from section to section, Griff laying a trail of ash from his cigarette onto the deck as he went. Their first stop was the passenger cabins, and Tory went in first, slamming open the door as if expecting to catch someone inside. Griff then watched as she methodically searched through the cupboards and drawers. However, all she found was an assortment of clothes, including an old blue-grey RAF boiler suit, plus various tools and random electronics.

"These are Liberty Devan's quarters," said Tory, stepping back outside the door. "There's nothing in here, especially not for you."

Griff squeezed past Tory and entered the room anyway. "I think I'll double check, just in case," he said, talking with the cigarette still in his mouth. He then began to sift through Liberty's clothes, while Tory looked on, her mouth puckered as if she had a slice of lemon on her tongue.

"Get out of there, you lecherous creep," said Tory, the disgust obvious in her voice. "There's nothing in there, like I told you."

Griff smiled up at Tory and stubbed out his cigarette on the table by the side of the bed. It burned a scorch mark into the polymer top. "I disagree," he said, grabbing one of Liberty's tank tops and then pressing it to his nose and inhaling deeply. "Mmm, delicious. It smells like desperation and bad life choices."

Tory snatched the top from Griff's hands and then yanked him out of the room, before pressing her forearm to his throat.

"Take it easy..." Griff spluttered, as Tory added pressure. "It was... a... joke..."

Tory released him and then stepped back, as Griff pushed himself away from the wall, rubbing his neck. "Shit, Tory, just whose side are you on, anyway?"

Tory's eyes remained locked on to Griff like a homing missile tracking its target. "I'm not on anyone's side, asshole," she growled, fists clenched tightly.

She was raging, and Griff realized then that he'd never actually seen Tory angry before. Not really. He'd seen her act pissed off, frustrated, apathetic, relentless and with a chilling, violent ruthlessness, but never angry. It scared the hell out of him.

Just then the ship began to shake, forcing them to grab onto the walls to steady themselves. The sense of danger took over, and both of them immediately ran towards the cockpit area to find Cutler. They met him in the living space, running the other way.

"Was that you?" Griff blurted out, "Why the hell have you powered up the ship?"

Cutler scowled, "I haven't, I thought it might have been something you did in engineering."

"We didn't get that far," answered Tory, before glowering at Griff.

Another tremor rumbled through the deck of the ship, shaking used whiskey glasses off the table in front of the semicircular couch.

"If it's not the ship then it's the station," said Cutler. "We must leave."

Cutler brushed past Griff, and Tory followed him, but Griff held his ground. "Hey, like I already told you, I give the orders around here," he barked. "We came to find the crystal, and we're not leaving without it."

"If they have hidden this crystal then it could take hours to locate it," answered Cutler. "That is time I do not believe we have. If these tremors are emanating from the station, it may already be unstable. And Hudson Powell will be returning soon."

Cutler again moved to leave, but Griff chased after him and grabbed his arm. Cutler glowered back at Griff, his face for once displaying some emotion, and Griff immediately let go. "If he's coming back then good," said Griff, taking a step away from Cutler. He'd only ever truly feared Tory, but now he saw that Cutler could be just as dangerously unpredictable. He needed to watch his step. "We wait for him to return, ambush him, and then force him to give us the crystal."

Cutler glanced at Tory, whose expression gave nothing away, and then back to Griff. "Fine, but once we have the crystal, I alone get to kill him, agreed?"

"I don't give a shit about Powell," said Griff. "Once we have the crystal, you can do whatever the hell you want with him."

"Agreed," said Cutler, before again turning to leave.

"The girl is mine, though," added Griff, remembering the idea he'd had back in the officer's mess on Deimos Station. Cutler and Tory both stopped and turned in almost perfect synchronization.

"What do you want with her, you disgusting piece of shit?" snapped Tory, resting a hand on her weapon.

"That is none of our concern," Cutler cut in, dismissing Tory's obvious distaste for Griff's proposal with a waft of his hand. Then he looked at Griff and added, in his sinister, flat drawl. "If you want to take the girl alive then that is your business. But it is not part of our bargain, and I will not help you."

"I don't need your help with her," said Griff, annoyed that Cutler was seeming to imply otherwise. "I just need for you not to kill her, that's all." Then he glanced at Tory, before looking back at Cutler. "A girl with her talents would be of great interest to certain organizations in the Outer Portal Worlds."

Tory looked ready to jump Griff, but then a violent quake suddenly rocked the ship, knocking them all to the deck. It rumbled on for several seconds, during which time Griff took cover underneath the table in front of the semicircular couch. When it finally eased, Cutler was quick to get up and move.

"This is madness! Staying here much longer is suicide," Cutler yelled, as Griff climbed out from underneath the table. The mercenary appeared genuinely rattled; another emotional state that was almost unheard of for Cutler. "If Powell doesn't return soon, there will be nothing left of him, or this station."

"We had a deal, Cutler," snarled Griff.

"And I will uphold it," Cutler replied. "But no part of that deal involved me dying on this space station. If Powell returns soon, then we take him. If not, we leave and await another opportunity."

This time Cutler did leave the living space, but Tory hung back, watching Griff like a hawk. Griff scowled at her and went to move past, but Tory held up her arm to stop him.

"Take the crystal," said Tory, with a quiet menace, "But, I don't care what Cutler said; touch a hair on her head, and I'll hunt you down myself."

As much as Griff found Tory nice to look at, he was weary of her constant, disrespectful attitude. Tory was under his employ. In fact, she wasn't even that – she was just the hired gun for the person under his employ. Griff called the shots, and he could do whatever the hell he liked.

"You'll do whatever Cutler tells you," he hit back, before pushing past Tory. Ordinarily, he wouldn't have dared put a hand on her, but she'd pissed him off past the point of rational decision-making. "And Cutler does whatever I tell him." Then he leveled a bony yellow finger at Tory. "You don't want me as an enemy, Tory. I know what you are, and I know what you were. And I can see to it that you're sent right back there!"

Tory looked about ready to shred Griff into chunks, but the last statement seemed to stun her into silence. Griff hadn't intended to let on he knew anything about Tory's indentured past, but she had riled him, and he'd let it slip out. Nevertheless, he'd definitely meant the threat. *It's about damn time Tory learned her place,* he told himself.

Tory Bellona remained silent, so Griff grasped the opportunity to leave, before she decided to use her antique revolver in anger. He reached the intersection, that cut off towards the docking ring, and glanced back at the mercenary. She was still in the living space, where he'd left her, as if Griff's words had temporarily paralyzed her body.

Another smaller tremor then vibrated through the deck plating, and Griff took one last look back at Tory, before running for the door. However, he wasn't sure if it was the vibration of the ship that was causing Tory to shake, or the rage bubbling inside her veins. And he didn't want to be around to find out.

CHAPTER 9

Hudson clutched onto the frame of the door as another tremor rumbled through the station. As much as he liked to joke about Liberty blowing things up, he doubted short-circuiting a few wires inside a door panel was enough to send an entire space station into meltdown. When he was confident the tremor had subsided, he quickly moved past Liberty, into what they had assumed to be a storage bay.

"This station has been shut down for who knows how long, before today," Hudson said, giving Liberty a reassuring rap on the shoulder as he passed. "We don't know anything about why it lost power to begin with, or how bad or extensive the damage is. You may be good at causing chaos, Liberty, but you didn't do this."

"Whatever you say, skipper..." replied Liberty, appearing relieved that Hudson hadn't blamed her for causing the quakes. She quickly followed him inside, and started to scour the racks and open lockers for valuable items.

"It was the alien crystal that triggered this station to power up," Hudson added. "I know you're more the betting type than I am, but I'd put money on that massive power surge being the cause of the instability, rather than your hotwiring trick."

"I hope you're right," replied Liberty, quickly pocketing a few smaller items. "Either way, I don't think we should wait around too long to find out what happens next."

Hudson pushed open the lids on a cluster of containers and peered inside, looking for familiar relics first. As he was doing this, another quake shook the deck, causing two containers on a higher level to fall. He dodged, narrowly avoiding being crushed, and then shook his head and blew out a thankful sigh. "This has stopped being fun," he called over to Liberty. "Let's just bag up what we have and get the hell off the station."

There was no complaint from Liberty, who quickly began to sift through the items dislodged from the last tremor. She tossed the valuable ones into her rucksack, being less discriminate than she'd ordinarily be. Meanwhile, Hudson started to fill his bag with anything he judged might have value. But he was more concerned with being fast than being choosy.

Another tremor hit, and this time it was strong enough to throw them both off their feet. "Okay, that's it, we're leaving," said Hudson, pulling the drawstring on his rucksack and clipping the flap shut.

"Just a couple more minutes; there's some good stuff in here," said Liberty, still busily sorting through the items that had spilled to the deck.

Hudson slung on his rucksack and crouched down in front of her, "Liberty, come on, there will be other scores," he said, this time with a cold seriousness. "I've got a bad feeling about this place. We need to get out."

Liberty dropped one last relic into her bag and fastened the flap shut, "Okay, but there's enough in here to buy us our own private docking garage back on Brahms Three."

"I never thought I'd miss Brahms Three's sweaty scavenger town," said Hudson, stepping back to the open door, "But I'll take it over this freezing deathtrap, any day."

Liberty smiled, but the instant Hudson stepped over the door threshold, a riot of gunshots rang out. Hudson dove back inside as bullets ricocheted off the walls and deck.

"Hudson!" Liberty cried out, and scrambled to his side, before hauling his body further into the safety of the storage bay.

"I'm okay, Liberty, I'm not hit," said Hudson, climbing to his knees. Then he quickly patted himself down to make sure. "At least I don't think so." Blood trickled from his head where it had scraped against the metal floor. He dabbed it with his hand, then he quickly peeked back outside. There were two men and a woman crouched at the far end of an adjacent corridor, steadily moving towards them.

"We've got three angry hunters, moving this way," said Hudson, drawing his pistol from the shoulder holster. "It's around about now that I really wish you were armed," he added. Then he glanced back and saw that Liberty had removed an object about the size of a sixteen-ounce coffee mug from the side pocket of her bag.

"I may not have a gun, but there are other ways to arm yourself," said Liberty. She then grabbed some strands of loose wire from inside a damaged panel next to the door.

"What do you have in mind?" asked Hudson, as more bullets pinged off the deck. He leaned out and fired two shots, forcing the three relic hunters to take cover again. They were now about twenty meters from the storage bay door.

"This is a power cell," said Liberty, while wrapping the wire around part of the object. "I've bypassed its internal fuse, so when I short it, this thing will blow like a grenade, and kick out a ton of smoke."

"Are you sure a grenade is the most sensible plan right now?" queried Hudson. He was thinking about how the station was already seemingly on the verge of blowing itself apart.

Before Liberty could answer, the floor and walls shook again, but this time the magnitude was severe enough to crack the deck and warp the walls. Hudson and Liberty grabbed on tightly to each other, as containers and parts of the ceiling tumbled down around them. When the quake subsided, they both looked up and saw fear reflected in one another's eyes.

"On second thoughts, throw the damned grenade!" cried Hudson, coughing and brushing dust from his hair.

Liberty completed the short circuit, then immediately tossed the cell around the side of the door. They heard frantic cries of, 'grenade!' from one of the hunters, and then an explosion cascaded through the deck, though compared to the recent seismic quakes, it produced only a mild shimmy.

"Go, I'll cover you!" shouted Hudson, slapping Liberty on the back. He then watched as she charged out into the rising plume of smoke, staying as low as possible. Hudson followed close behind, aiming into the thick smog. Shots rang out and he dove to the deck, as more quakes, like aftershocks, started to shake the station. Hudson saw one of the hunters emerge from the smoke, weapon angled towards Liberty, and he fired instinctively, hitting the man in the leg. The hunter fell heavily, then was dragged back into the smoke, as if a monster's tentacle had ensnared him.

Hudson tried to get to his feet, but the deck was still shaking, making it almost impossible to maintain his balance. Liberty was already at the entrance to the next corridor, urging him on, but as Hudson staggered forward, one of the other hunters ran out and tackled him. Hudson fell and the pistol flew from his hands, spinning away in the direction he had been running. He took a punch to the ribs, but then fought back, as the hunter tried to wrestle his rucksack off him.

"What are you doing?!" Hudson yelled, grappling the man to the deck. "This station is tearing itself apart. We have to get out of here!"

The man steadied himself, resting on one knee with both palms pressed to the quivering deck plates. "I've risked too much coming here to leave with nothing," he snarled. "Give me that bag, and we'll let you leave unharmed."

The female hunter then staggered out of the rapidly dispersing cloud of smoke. She was trying to aim her pistol at Hudson, but the uneven motion of the deck meant that the barrel was waving around, as if she was drunk.

"Just give us the bag," the woman demanded, as another minor quake almost knocked her from her feet.

Suddenly Liberty appeared out of nowhere, having sprinted the distance with the silent agility of a cat. The female hunter turned the weapon on her, but Liberty struck it from her hand. She then spun on her heels and drove a swift kick into the female hunter's gut, sending her tumbling to the ground. There was another wicked shimmy, but Hudson managed to grab the male hunter, and use him as an anchor. The man squirmed under Hudson's weight, then slid out from beneath him as the quake subsided. Hudson rose to his feet first, kicking the man in the face, as if he was attempting to score a field goal with his head.

Leaving the dazed relic hunter trio behind, Hudson and Liberty darted for the corridor leading back to the Orion. Hudson saw his pistol on the deck and stooped down to collect it, letting Liberty draw ahead. He glanced back, seeing the hunters re-group and head off in the opposite direction. He smiled, then ran harder after Liberty, turning the corner seconds after she had.

"It's okay, they're heading the other way!" he called out, but then almost crashed into Liberty, who was standing motionless in the corridor. Hudson barely avoided colliding with her, and was about to yell at her, asking why she'd stopped running. However, as his eyes flicked beyond Liberty to another trio of figures standing in the passage, the answer became clear. Blocking their path back to the Orion were Tory Bellona and Cutler Wendell. And they were accompanied by Logan Griff.

CHAPTER 10

Cutler Wendell stepped forward, maintaining a steady aim with his weapon, despite the now constant tremors that shook the station. He glanced down at the pistol in Hudson's hand, then locked eyes with him.

"Don't try anything foolish," Cutler warned, while switching his aim to Liberty. "I can kill the girl and wound you, before you could get a single shot off."

Hudson noticed Griff scowl at Cutler, then move to the mercenary's side. He looked like he was about to say something to Cutler, but he held his tongue, and turned to Hudson instead.

"We want the alien crystal, rook," said Griff, also raising his weapon. "Just hand it over, and we'll let both of you fly out of here."

Hudson shook his head, "What crystal? I don't know what..."

"Save it, rook," Griff interrupted as another tremor forced them all momentarily off balance. "I know you have it. If we have to, we'll kill you and search for it ourselves."

"Looks like you've already tried that," said Liberty, noticing that the outer hatch light was green, indicating the hatch was unlocked. "But you won't get it without our help, and we all know there's no time before this station blows."

"Then we come with you," said Cutler, again asserting control over the conversation. "Inspector Griff and I will accompany Mr. Powell on the VCX-110." Then he aimed the weapon at Liberty again. "The girl goes with Tory, as insurance so that you don't try to double-cross us."

"Like hell, I'm not going anywhere with that psychopath," snarled Liberty. Suddenly, a sharp crack cut through the constant background rumble, as Cutler Wendell fired. The report of the weapon made Hudson jolt back in surprise, but he also instinctively knew what Cutler had done. Twisting sharply to face Liberty, his partner stumbled towards him and grasped his shoulders tightly. He felt panic grip his body as Liberty's weight was transferred to him, and he saw blood running down her leg.

"You bastard!" Hudson cried out, as Liberty pressed her hand over her wounded thigh, moaning through gritted teeth.

"She'll live," snarled Cutler, his usually soulless expression betraying anger and resentment. "But unless you give me the crystal, the next bullet will be to her head."

"Back off, Cutler," growled Griff, pushing down on Cutler's arm to force his weapon down. "I told you, I want the girl alive." Cutler brushed Griff off and pushed him back, before again thrusting the weapon towards Liberty.

"Now, Powell!" Cutler roared. "The crystal or she dies!"

"Okay, okay!" Hudson yelled back. His eyes briefly flicked across to Griff, who appeared to be both stunned and furious at Cutler's forceful dismissal of him. Glancing back to Cutler, it seemed clear that the mercenary had become unhinged. He had no choice but to do what he asked. "I'll give you the damn crystal. But it's on the ship, and there's no time to get it now!"

The fury had now surfaced fully from wherever Cutler Wendell kept his emotions locked away. It was seeping to the surface like pus from a wound, and there was no stopping its bitter flow.

"Then time is up for your friend too..." Cutler sneered, before lifting his weapon and aiming it at Liberty's head.

A shot rang out and Hudson squeezed Liberty tightly, trying to shield her with his own body. However, neither Liberty nor himself was hit. Hudson glanced back and saw that Tory had deflected Cutler's aim, pushing his hand up, so that the bullet hit the ceiling. Griff looked on, appearing as surprised by Tory's intervention as Cutler was.

"She's not part of the agreement," snarled Tory, with an icy assertiveness. "You're losing focus. Kill her and our deal with Griff goes south, for me as well as you."

Cutler slapped her hand away and stepped back, glaring at Tory with feral eyes. For a moment, Hudson thought Cutler and Tory were going to come to blows, but before anything could happen, another quake rocked the station. This time it was powerful enough to throw everyone off their feet and to the deck. The corridor started to twist and buckle, and atmosphere began to bleed out of fractures in the walls. Then the station's gravity failed.

Hudson held on to Liberty and grabbed a torn panel of deck plating to keep them rooted, while Tory, Griff and Cutler were sent pinballing off the walls. Then as suddenly as it had switched off, the gravity generators kicked back in. Tory dropped the full height of the corridor, and landed heavily, while Cutler and Griff were spared harder falls. However, both men were still badly winded, and lay sprawled out on their backs.

Hudson seized the opportunity and charged, drop-kicking Cutler Wendell in the back as he rose. The mercenary cartwheeled down the corridor, dropping his weapon in the process, before cracking his head against the deck. He climbed unsteadily to his feet, cast his eyes back to Tory, lying motionless on the deck, then to Hudson. Then he ran.

"Coward!" roared Hudson, but then Griff pounced and struck Hudson across the face with the back of his fist. However, Hudson barely felt the impact. Adrenalin was now surging through his veins. Combined with his own rage at seeing Liberty get shot, it would take an army of Griffs to hold him back. He stepped in and hammered Griff with a succession of brutal punches to the head and body, sending him down again. Then, standing over his prone body, Hudson grabbed a tuft of his stringy black hair and forced Griff to look at him. Griff met Hudson's gaze with bloodshot eyes, before Hudson pulled back his fist, ready to strike. He wanted to do it. He wanted to pummel the bastard so hard that his nose collapsed into his skull. Yet as the station trembled around them, Hudson hesitated from dealing the final blow.

"You don't have the guts, rook," laughed Griff, spitting blood onto the deck. "You never did. You're weak, and that's why I'll always beat you."

Hudson gritted his teeth and clenched his fist more tightly. It was taking everything he had not to smash Griff's worthless face into the wall.

"Hudson!"

The cry came from Liberty. Still holding tightly onto Griff's hair, Hudson looked back to see her limping towards him, using the wall for support. She had wrapped an emergency bandage around her wound. Hudson remembered that they'd carried them in their packs – another item that Tory had thrown into Hudson's trolley in the Scavenger's Paradise on Bach Two. He was glad Liberty had the presence of mind to use the emergency supplies. However, he also felt a sudden rush of guilt that he'd left her to fend for herself, while blind rage had compelled him to attack Griff.

"He's not worth it, Hudson," Liberty said, as she got closer.

"Listen to your pet, rook," said Griff, smiling, but then a sharp jab from Liberty's right hand silenced him.

"You're not worth it, because he's a better man than you'll ever be," Liberty spat, glowering down at him. "One day you'll get what's coming to you, but we aren't killers." Then she looked up at Hudson, eyes imploring him. "Right?"

Hudson dropped Griff, then picked up the RGF officer's weapon. He applied the safety and slid it down the waistband of his pants. "That's right," he answered, though he was looking at Liberty when he said it, rather than Griff. Then Hudson took a pace back and kicked Griff further down the corridor. "Go on, get out of my sight, before I change my mind."

Griff struggled to his feet and staggered away from Hudson. "You'll always be gutless, rook," he said, wiping blood from his mouth. "Gutless and dumb. And don't think for a second this is over." Then Griff started to stagger away down the corridor, struggling against the now chaotic motion of the station, which was growing more unstable by the second. Hudson and Liberty watched him like hawks, until he finally rounded a corner and was gone.

CHAPTER 11

Hudson let out a weary sigh and pressed his hands to his hips. "Why do I get the feeling we're going to regret letting that asshole go?" he said, before helping Liberty to the threshold of the Orion's docking port.

"Don't get me wrong, I'd love to have seen you pummel Griff into dust," said Liberty, hobbling inside the ship. "But not killing him was the right thing to do."

Hudson nodded, "The right thing to do, but maybe not the smart thing to do," he replied, ominously. Then he glanced back out into the corridor to make sure Griff was definitely gone, and his heart leapt as he spotted Tory still lying on the deck. She was moving, but appeared heavily dazed. Hudson turned back to Liberty and quickly checked her wound, which was no longer bleeding. "Can you make it to the cockpit, and get the ship ready to launch?" he asked, urgently.

"I can, but why, where the hell are you going?" replied Liberty. Then she too saw Tory on the deck. She grabbed Hudson's shoulders, holding him back. "Hudson, come on, we don't have time for this!"

Hudson darted inside, grabbed an emergency medical kit, then met Liberty's despondent eyes. "What were you just telling me about doing the right thing?" he said, using Liberty's own advice against her.

"And what did you just tell me about the right thing not always being the smart thing?" Liberty replied, her responses, as ever, as sharp as her wits.

"She saved you, Liberty, I can't just leave her," Hudson said, firmly. He'd made up his mind. Then he pointed to Liberty's leg. "That bandage will clot the blood and stop any further bleeding." Then he opened the medical kit and removed a jet syringe, before holding it up to Liberty. "And this will keep you on your feet till I can treat it more closely."

Liberty scowled at the device, then at Hudson, before shooting him a resigned nod. "Did I ever mention that Tory Bellona would be the death of you?" she said, as Hudson pressed the jet syringe to her neck. There was a hiss and Liberty flinched briefly as the drugs were injected into her bloodstream.

"Yes, I think you did mention it, once or twice..." Hudson replied, smiling. Then his eyes hardened again. "Get the ship started, I won't be long." Then he turned to leave, but hesitated, and again met Liberty's eyes. "But, if it looks like the station is going to collapse, and I'm not here, just go without me, got it?"

Liberty grabbed a fistful of Hudson's dark leather jacket, "Don't be a moron, Hudson," she replied. Oddly, the words came across with surprising tenderness. "I'm not going anywhere without you." Then she pushed him away, out towards the corridor and Tory. "Now go help her, while there's still time.

Hudson nodded, then raced out into the trembling corridor, before sliding to his knees at Tory's side. She was now on her back, holding her head, but appeared more alert. He quickly checked her over, finding no obvious broken bones, then opened the medical kit.

"Tory, if you can hear me, I'm going to give you a shot," said Hudson, preparing another jet syringe. "It will give you a sudden burst of energy and alertness, but will also leave you with one hell of a hangover..."

Hudson applied the syringe and almost instantly Tory jolted upright, screaming like a banshee. She grabbed Hudson by the back of the neck, while pressing the palm of her hand to his throat. Hudson spluttered, but was unable to speak, and then

Tory's wild eyes recognized him, and she released her hold.

"What happened?" asked Tory, squeezing her eyes shut from the pain. "Where's Cutler?"

"That cowardly piece of shit ran," said Hudson. "He left you here to die."

Tory scrambled to her feet and looked around, before wincing again. "What the hell did you just give me?"

"It's called a concussion drug," said Hudson, removing another item out of the medical kit. "I don't know how it works; I just know it gets you off your ass faster than an ejector seat. The RGF trained me how to use them." Then he pressed the second item from the medical kit into Tory's hand. "When its effects wear off, take this for the pain and nausea."

Tory opened her hand and then shot a confused frown at Hudson. "Cutler left me here?"

"Yeah, the guy is an asshole," said Hudson, and then added, sarcastically, "Who would have figured?"

"He wouldn't have left me," said Tory, shaking her head. She still appeared to be in a slight daze.

Hudson held Tory's shoulders, and she met his eyes, appearing more alert. "Tory, this station is about to rip itself apart, we have to leave," he said. "Come with me, I'll get you out of here."

Tory looked up at him, but then shook her head again. "No, I need to get back to my ship." She pulled away from Hudson, and started to get her bearings. "He wouldn't leave me."

"Tory, wake up, he left you to die!" Hudson called over to her, as she staggered away. "Just come with me."

Tory shook her head again. "No, he wouldn't leave me," she repeated, her voice now raised to a yell. "Not after everything I've done for him!"

"Tory!" Hudson shouted, but the mercenary was running now, down the twisted corridor, and back towards Cutler's FS-31. "Tory!" Hudson cried again, running after her. He squinted against the flashing lights, but she was already gone.

Then the station shook again, and more cracks appeared in the walls. Atmosphere was now bleeding into space far more rapidly, and Hudson could feel fluctuations in the gravity field. It was like being on a rollercoaster, as it climbed and fell over a long series of humps, but without actually moving.

"Shit!" Hudson cried out, angry that Tory still could not tear herself away from Cutler's vice-like hold on her. He turned and ran back to the Orion, before swinging inside and slamming the button to close the hatch. The heavy metal door began to close, but Hudson was already sprinting through the ship to the cockpit. He found Liberty in the second seat, leg up on the dash. All the Orion's systems were online and ready.

"What the hell took you so long?!" she shouted, as Hudson threw off his pack and jumped into the pilot's seat.

"That woman is so damn stubborn," growled Hudson, flipping an array of switches and grabbing the controls.

"Sounds like someone else I know..." said Liberty, looking at him out of the corner of her eye. Then she grabbed a lever on her right side. "Detaching... now!"

Hudson felt the docking clamp detach and thrusted hard away from the station. Lining the nose up with the comforting sea of stars at the far end of the docking bay, he then rammed the throttle lever forward. The kick of the engines was ferocious. Hudson glanced left and saw other hunter ships detaching, but one was caught in an explosion as the station began its final death throes.

"This is going to be close," said Hudson as they shot out of the bay into space, like a bullet from a rifle.

"It already is close!" shouted Liberty, as a flash of light lit up the cockpit.

They felt the shockwave hit, then alarms rang out all around them. Hudson saw several warning lights flash on, but there were too many to take stock of.

"We've taken some damage," he said, quickly surveying his consoles. "I don't know how bad."

Then they heard the cockpit door lock, and the lights dimmed and turned red.

"Shit, we're losing environmental systems," said Liberty, who was also franticly checking her screens. "The cockpit has been sealed off as an emergency measure. We maybe only have an hour of oxygen in here."

Hudson hammered his fist onto the arm of the chair, "Damn it, that's nowhere near enough to get back to Deimos."

"We're going to have to set down on the planet for repairs," added Liberty, "I'm afraid we're not done with this system yet."

Hudson sighed and cut the main drives, before pulsing the thrusters to bring the dying space station into view. Dozens of explosions rippled throughout the entirety of the massive structure, sending chunks of metal into space. Another explosion pushed the fractured alien wreck out from its resting place. Despite the violence of the explosions going off around it, and the impacts from debris, its thick alien armor resisted further damage. It again made Hudson wonder – and worry – what sort of ship could have taken it down in the first place.

"That's not something you see every day," said Liberty, shaking her head in awe.

Hudson was no longer looking at the unique spectacle outside; he was staring down at the navigation scanner. Two ships had perished in the escape, but the interference from the explosions was preventing a clear ID reading on the remaining vessels.

"Did she get out?" asked Liberty, causing Hudson to look up. She'd asked the question with genuine concern and sensitivity. "Tory, I mean... did she get out?"

Hudson sighed again, engaged the main drives and steered them on a course towards the planet.

"I don't know," he admitted, offering Liberty a weak smile. "But I hope so."

CHAPTER 12

The shockwave from the detonation of the alien space station had damaged both Logan Griff's RGF Patrol Craft and Cutler Wendell's FS-31. Both had agreed a rendezvous on the planet's surface, about a kilometer distant from the severed half of the alien wreck. Its counterpart, set free during the explosion of the station, was now in a decaying orbit. One day, it too would smash into the surface and become a hive for relic hunters looking to make their fortune.

The damage to Griff's vessel had not been extensive. This was a lucky break, considering the relative fragility of his RGF Patrol Craft compared to most other ships. With the assistance of Cutler and Tory, he estimated that the patch-ups could be made in only a couple of hours, once they were on the ground.

Cutler's FS-31 had fared slightly less well, on account of the mercenary's last-second departure. After their heated exchange on the space station, Griff had expected there to be some tension between Cutler and Tory. However, as soon as they had met up at the rendezvous, it was clear to Griff that their relationship had soured. There was anger, bitterness and even resentment between them now, though it all bubbled under the surface, like magma beneath a volcano. It was because of this that Griff had held back from confronting Cutler about losing control on the station. He didn't want to tip the mercenary over the edge, and have him snap on him, instead of Tory.

After assisting with the repairs to the RGF Patrol Craft, Cutler had left Tory to work on the FS-31, and remained with Griff. This in itself was unusual, Griff had thought. He and Cutler Wendell had always had a strong working relationship, based on mutual benefits. Yet Griff had been under no illusion that Cutler liked him, or considered him a friend. Not that Griff cared either way. However, after Cutler had so brusquely shrugged him off on the station, while he was threatening Liberty Devan, Griff been left with no doubts as to Cutler's true opinion of him. Taking this into account, Griff was curious as to why the mercenary had chosen to pass the time with him, as opposed to his trained attack dog. And it was a mystery he intended to get to the bottom of.

Griff stepped down from the repair platform and deactivated it, causing it to slide back into its housing in the hull. He turned to Cutler, but he was staring off towards the alien wreck, seemingly lost in his own thoughts. Griff also thought for a moment, then stepped into the cargo hold. He unclipped and then opened the supplies container, before taking out a beer for himself. Alcohol was prohibited on RGF vessels, but his private stash was another perk of Griff's new position. He then dug deeper into the cooler and found a bottle of water. He knew that Cutler didn't drink alcohol, and considered that the water might act as an ice breaker. He had no desire to make friends with the man; quite the opposite – he didn't give two shits how Cutler felt. He merely hoped that the peace offering would loosen his tongue enough to find out what really happened on the station, after they had been split up.

Griff sidled up beside Cutler and held out the water, without speaking a word. For a few seconds they both stood side-by-side, looking at the wreck, with the water bottle hanging in the air. Then Cutler met Griff's eyes, looked at the bottle and, also without a word, took it. The mercenary popped open the cap and took a polite sip, before finally breaking the silence.

"Thank you, Inspector."

"Repairs to my ship are pretty much complete," said Griff, after taking a swig of his beer. He intended to play it casual, and not bring up Tory, in the hope that Cutler would do it himself. "We were lucky to escape that station in one piece."

"Did you detect Hudson Powell's vessel?" Cutler replied, choosing not to engage with Griff's attempts to make conversation. "Did your scanner pick up his vessel, after you departed?"

Griff shook his head, "No, that station was kicking out far too much EM interference."

Cutler was silent for a few seconds, during which time he took staccato sips from the bottle of water, like an anxious bird drinking from a pond. "If Powell did not survive then I still expect to be compensated for my time so far."

Griff almost laughed out loud. *Mercs and relic hunters... Scum, the lot of them. Always out for whatever they can take,* he thought. Normally he would have shot Cutler down, but he didn't want to antagonize him, at least not until he'd revealed more information.

"Hudson Powell may be an idiot, but luck seems to follow him," Griff replied. "I'm sure he survived. But if not, the RGF will compensate you for your efforts so far."

This appeared to appease Cutler. However, Griff couldn't resist the urge to add a thornier postscript to his last statement. And now that Cutler seemed unlikely to snap and kill him in a fit of rage, he decided to beat his chest a little. "Though if you go back on your word to me again, I'll make sure the

RGF takes a far keener interest in your activities in the future."

Cutler glanced over to Griff briefly, but Griff didn't meet his gaze. He continued to stare out imperiously at the wreck, drinking his beer. He had to reassert his authority over the mercenary. He had to know he could still trust him. Or at least trust that the mercenary would follow his orders.

"I apologize for what happened on the station," said Cutler, and Griff had to fight hard to suppress a smile. "Hudson Powell has evaded me too many times. I am not accustomed to being made of fool of. Those that defy me end up dead."

"You'll get him soon enough," said Griff, satisfied that he was again the alpha in the relationship. "And when I get that crystal, and the RGF finds a bunch of new portal worlds, we'll both be rich. We'll be rich, and Hudson Powell will be dead."

"What did you intend to do with the girl, Liberty Devan?" asked Cutler.

The question came out of nowhere, and caught Griff off guard. He had purposely been holding back on personal queries until the right moment, and hadn't expected to get asked one of his own. "Not what *she* thought I had in mind," Griff answered, nodding in the direction of Cutler's ship. It seemed like a good opportunity to bring Tory into the conversation. "Though, don't get me wrong, I wouldn't mind some bunk time with her."

"Then what?" Cutler asked again. There was no hint of an accusation; Cutler had again buried his emotions deep down.

"That little bitch has slighted me one too many times," said Griff, lacking Cutler's emotional composure. "So, I'm going to sell her to one of the shittier corporations out in OPW space. Maybe even to the Council itself. That will teach her a lesson, and see me with a nice bounty to boot."

Cutler nodded. "I understand."

Griff's attention was then diverted by the sound of boots crunching on the rocky soil of the desert planet. He turned around to see Tory Bellona approaching. She stopped about five meters away, and appeared even more standoffish than usual.

"The repairs are complete," said Tory, ignoring Griff. "We can leave." Then her expression hardened like the stone under her feet. "Don't forget to wait for me this time."

Griff's eyes widened; the atmosphere between the two mercenaries was taut, like a tripwire. Cutler walked towards Tory, clearly uneasy at Griff's proximity, and tried to usher her away. However, Tory appeared in no mood to be placated, and she also wasn't going to be moved.

"I wouldn't have left you," said Cutler, trying to keep his voice hushed. However, the wind was in a favorable direction, and Griff could hear every word. He turned his back to the pair, in a feigned attempt to give them privacy, but Griff's keen ears were still listening intently.

"But you did leave me," said Tory, not even attempting to hush her words. "You left me unconscious on the floor of that damned alien station, while it was tearing itself apart."

"I didn't realize you were hurt," Griff heard Cutler reply. Yet there was no emotion in his voice, and his monotone delivery sounded unconvincing, even to Griff. "I was waiting for you on the ship. I was still there when you returned, was I not?"

"Yes, you were still there," Tory conceded, but even though Griff couldn't see her face, he could tell she wasn't being swayed by Cutler's words. "But whether you were waiting for me, or just struggling to take off without me, I can't say."

Griff now remembered that Tory had been lying on the floor of the corridor, when he and Hudson Powell had fought. In the frantic moments after Hudson had let him leave, he'd forgotten all about her. However, Tory was right; Cutler had fled and left her to die, despite his protestations to the contrary.

Griff thought for a moment. A rift between Cutler and Tory was bad for business, he realized. Tory was already unpredictable, but he'd believed Cutler's assertions that she was loyal. If the status quo between the two hunters was changing, then Tory was a threat to his mission. Griff knew in that moment that she'd have to go, but how and when was a problem for another time.

During Griff's moments of reflection, there had been silence behind him, and so he chanced a look around. The relic hunter mercenaries both met his eyes, then broke apart, Tory still looking like a thundercloud that was about to erupt.

As if perfectly planned to break the tension, Griff's wristpad chimed an alert. He read the message, which had been relayed from his ship's computer, and laughed out loud.

"What the hell is so funny?" snapped Tory. One thing that hadn't altered was her prickly attitude towards Griff.

"Always so touchy...." Griff hit back, sneering at her. "But if you must know, Hudson Powell's ship has just landed. I think it's funny that the dumb prick keeps coming back for more."

"Landed where?" asked Cutler, driving straight to the point.

"About fifty kilometers away, up on that ridge behind the wreck," said Griff, pointing in the general direction. "I guess he must need to make repairs too."

"Then there is no time to lose," said Cutler, immediately turning back towards his ship. "We can come in low, and keep the ridge between us and his vessel. Then attack his landing site on foot. With luck, he will not see us coming." Then Cutler seemed to notice Griff was scowling at him. "Assuming you approve, of course, Inspector."

Griff smiled. Cutler was back on the leash, at least for now. "Plan approved..." he said, but then added, more pointedly, "but be sure that you stick to the terms of our bargain this time." The mercenary returned a respectful nod, and started jogging back to his ship.

Griff also turned to leave, but then noticed Tory was still there. He turned to her, frowning. "Something else you wanted to say?"

"What do you want with the girl?" said Tory, tersely.

Griff's eyes narrowed, "That's none of your concern. Just do what you're hired to do, and stay out of my business, or..." Griff hesitated. His success in taming Cutler had gone to his head, and he'd overstepped with Tory. He knew that threatening her was never a good idea.

"Or what, asshole?" snarled Tory, resting a hand on the grip of her six-shooter.

Griff clenched his teeth so hard that his jaw started to hurt. He wanted to put Tory in her place, just as he had done to Cutler, but he didn't want to catch a bullet for his trouble.

"Just do your job, Tory," Griff said, choosing discretion over valor. "Or I'll find someone else who will."

CHAPTER 13

Hudson stood on the ridge and stared out at the fractured alien wreck, smashed into the rocks far in the distance below him. He'd seen many wrecks before, but none like this one. Torn in half along the center line, Hudson could see the maze of hexagonal corridors and cavernous internal spaces in a totally different light. It had already been understood that the alien hulks were largely giant engines and reactors, but even so, seeing it cut open was a revelation. It made it seem even more alien, somehow.

There were now six RGF vessels dotted around the hulk, and work had already begun to establish the checkpoint perimeter. Hudson wondered what the other hunter crews had discovered inside, and how many were yet to emerge. He thought back to Percy Harrison, the intrepid hunter who had perished inside the wreck on Bach

Two, and wondered if any of the hunters below would share a similar fate. He had always known that relic hunting was a perilous occupation. Even so, Hudson had perhaps underestimated just how dangerous it could be. Yet, despite this, he wasn't discouraged. The things he'd seen and done in the short space of time since meeting Liberty had been the most exhilarating of his life. He'd finally found something he truly cared about. As well as someone.

He glanced back to check on Liberty, who was still working to repair the damage to the Orion. Hudson's RGF training had included what was essentially battlefield medicine, and he'd been able to treat Liberty's wound successfully. Thanks to a combination of advanced healing accelerants and rapid tissue repair treatments, Liberty was already on her feet. Though it would be a few days before she was back to her ninja-kicking best.

"How are the repairs coming along?" asked Hudson, hopping over the craggy rocks around their landing site and peering up at the Orion.

"Maybe another hour," replied Liberty, without looking up from her datapad. She was directing a small fleet of repair automatons, which were doing the bulk of the work. "I've fixed the environmental systems, but the shockwave from the explosion hit us pretty hard, and I want to make sure everything is still bolted and sealed up tight. I wouldn't want to risk a fuel line blowing on us at one-g, while we're flying back to Mars." Then she pointed up at the aft hull plating. "Our alien-infused armor saved our skins though. And, even better, it pretty much repairs itself."

Hudson nodded and smiled. Liberty was clearly enjoying herself. He'd almost forgotten that her primary occupation, prior to galivanting around the galaxy with Hudson, was patching up and fixing space ships. "Roger that, I think I'm going to wander further along the ridge," said Hudson. "I want to get another angle on that hulk down there."

"Whatever you say, skipper," replied Liberty, "I'll be right here, doing all the hard work."

Hudson laughed, "You really don't want me fixing this thing. I'll just make it worse."

Liberty smiled and then waved him off with a sort of 'shoo' gesture. It was the kind of thing you might do to get rid of an annoying pigeon that was trying to steal your lunch.

Hudson took his cue to leave and started to scramble along the rocky landscape. The planet, like so many portal worlds, was largely barren. There was some evidence of vegetative life – a smattering of trees and the occasional oasis – but in general it was stark and empty. It reminded Hudson of the Colorado Desert in California.

He continued on for perhaps ten or fifteen minutes, until he came to a strange, hollowed-out section in the ridge. It looked like a giant had taken a long scoop out of the rock and earth with an enormous spoon. The sides of the hollow looked strange, as if they were shimmering. He looked closer, and noticed that the soil and looser rocks were steadily falling towards the center, like sand through an hourglass. He knelt down and pressed the palm of his hand to the rock and felt a vibration. It was subtle enough that he hadn't picked up on it through the thick soles of his boots. However, now that he was more attuned to the sensation, it felt like the entire ridge was quavering gently.

"What the hell is going on?" he wondered, talking out loud into the warm, dry breeze. He stood up, considering that perhaps Liberty had started the Orion's engines, but then something caught his attention down in the scoop. There was a metallic glint from an object that was concealed just beneath the loose surface rocks at the far side of the ravine. He scrambled down the side and moved closer, starting to feel a tightening in his gut. It was a similar sensation to the one he had experienced after discovering the alien shuttle on Zimmer One. *Maybe it's another Morphus?* Hudson wondered, as he moved closer to the object. Tentatively, he dug out some of the rocks to reveal a smooth, black surface. It was an alien metal, similar to the sort used on the outer hull of the wrecks.

He dug away more of the rocks until he began to reveal the shape of the object. It was smooth, angular and definitely not natural. However, his first assumption that it was another being like Morphus didn't seem to be accurate. Hudson didn't recall the alien shuttle having such a razor-sharp edge to its design, and this ship – if it was a ship – seemed much smaller too. The tight feeling in his gut remained. He'd learned his lesson from Zimmer One; this time, he wasn't going to go snooping around. He'd got lucky awakening the Morphus being, as it had, so far at least, turned out to be benign. He wasn't going to roll the dice again, and take a chance on whatever this new thing was being hostile.

Suddenly, the ridge began to tremble more violently, and Hudson rapidly backed away as loose soil began to bury his feet. Heart pounding, he frantically scrambled up out of the hollow. The tremors were growing in severity now, and Hudson was forced to grab onto a large rock that was jutting out of the surface in order to stop from falling. Then he heard the unmistakable roar of starship engines powering up, and slowly the mass of stones in the scoop started to rise.

"Oh shit, not again!" Hudson yelled, as he watched an alien ship slowly rise from its rocky grave, clinging on to the rock for dear life. He wasn't convinced that this time it was his meddling that had awakened the vessel, but he was sure Liberty wouldn't see it that way.

The vessel hung in the air a few meters above the ridge, showering Hudson with dust and earth that was falling from its hull. Hudson was paralyzed to the spot. All he could do was clutch the rock and watch. However, now it was obvious that this was not the same type of vessel as the one belonging to Morphus. It was definitely smaller – about the size of an RGF Patrol Craft – and its angular shape gave it a meaner, more sinister appearance.

The vessel continued to hang in the air, mere meters from where Hudson was still cowering behind his shield of rock. The difference was that now it was turning sharply from side-to-side, as if it were a head on an invisible swivel. Then the glow from its engines intensified and it accelerated upwards at a ferocious velocity.

The downdraught from the ship's engines sent Hudson soaring backwards, as if he'd been shot from a giant catapult. His arms and legs flailed desperately in an attempt to control his fall, but he was at the mercy of the planet's Earth-normal gravity. He raised his arms to shield his face and then landed awkwardly in a patch of dense weeds. The momentum of the fall carried him on, and he felt his head slam into something solid. He groaned and then his eyes went dark, while the distant roar of the alien vessel's engines faded to nothing.

CHAPTER 14

Hudson opened his eyes, and straight away had to shield them against the blazing light from the planet's orange sun. Groggily at first, he pushed himself up and saw that he'd come to rest in a patch of dense, grassy vegetation. A couple of meters to either side and he'd likely have been killed, smashed against the sharper, bare rocks.

There was no sign of the alien vessel that had risen out of its rocky grave like an undead warrior. All that remained was the crater where it had slept. For some reason, it had chosen this moment to reanimate from its hibernation. *Perhaps it was triggered by the crystal, like the space station?* Hudson thought, dabbing blood from the back of his head.

Hudson started to make his way back along the ridge to the Orion, to let Liberty know what had happened. He considered it unlikely that Liberty wouldn't have also spotted the angular alien ship blasting off. Yet he was surprised not to see her out and about, looking for him.

Hudson's progress was slow at first, as he still felt dazed from the fall. However, the cool, fresh air on the ridge invigorated him, and he soon began to feel stronger again. About twenty minutes after setting off, he eventually reached the plateau on the ridge where he'd set down the Orion, but Liberty was no longer outside.

"Liberty?" Hudson called out, approaching the ship cautiously, but there was no answer. "Liberty, are you there?"

He continued on, but something about the situation felt wrong. He expected Liberty to have charged out to meet him, fueled by a heady mix of excitement and fear. Then he noticed that the repair automatons were still sitting on the hull, buzzing with energy, but clearly with no instructions to act on. Liberty wouldn't have just left them out, Hudson realized. Something had happened to her, which meant danger was near.

Hudson reached inside his jacket and drew his pistol, stepping steadily around the side of the ship towards the opposite edge of the ridge. He tried to move with stealth, but each crunch of his boots on the dry, stony soil was unbearably loud. Then, as he cleared the ship and reached the far side of the ridge, he saw Liberty and froze. She was on her knees, blood trickling from her mouth and nose.

Behind her were Cutler Wendell and Tory Bellona, and standing to Liberty's side, hand tightened into a fist, was Logan Griff.

Cutler saw Hudson and immediately raised his weapon, but Hudson was alert enough to dart behind a cluster of rocks and take cover.

"Come on, rook," he heard Griff call out. "There's no point hiding back there. We have your pet, and if you want her back, you'll do as I say."

"If you want the crystal then let her go," Hudson called back, peeking around the side of the rocks. "Let her go and I'll give you what you want."

Griff smiled and then jabbed Liberty smartly across the side of her face.

"You bastard, I said I'll give you what you want!" shouted Hudson.

"You do what I say, rook," Griff answered, coolly. "And for every time you don't, I punch your little pet here."

Hudson gritted his teeth. He wanted to storm out from behind the rocks and fill the miserable, low-life coward with bullets. However, he knew that even if he did manage to kill Griff, Cutler would gun him down next, and then he'd likely kill Liberty too. He hated it, but he had no choice other than to do what Griff demanded.

"Fine, I'll do what you ask," Hudson called back.

Griff jabbed Liberty again, and Hudson saw her rock back from the blow. Cutler caught Liberty's shoulders, preventing her fall, and then propped her upright, his face displaying its usual lack of emotion. Liberty's eyes were half-closed, and the blood was flowing more freely now.

"Stop hitting her, damn you – I said I'd do what you ask!" Hudson yelled, but Griff just smiled.

"That one was just for my amusement," Griff said, wiping blood from his knuckle onto his pants. "Now throw down your weapon, go inside your crappy little ship and get me that crystal."

Hudson threw his pistol into the dirt in view of Griff, and then stepped out with his hands raised. "If I get you the crystal, will you let us go?"

Griff smiled again, clearly relishing his moment of triumph over Hudson. "I'll tell you what, rook," he began, "seeing as I'm feeling generous, I'll let one of you go free. You get to choose who lives and who dies."

"Fine, then let Liberty go," replied Hudson. He didn't want to play Griff's sick game, but if there was a chance even one of them could walk out of this alive, he had to try. Then he had an idea. Griff's word was worthless, and he doubted Cutler had any sense of honor either, but there was one person amongst them he knew did. He looked at Tory Bellona, who met his eyes with unblinking intensity. "Are we all agreed?"

Griff laughed, "This isn't a democracy, rook." Then he shrugged. "But, sure, fetch me the crystal, and your pet here walks free." Then he pointed his bony finger at Hudson. "You, on the other hand, get to turn to dust on this crappy, lifeless rock. That's a better death than you deserve."

Hudson started to walk towards the rear ramp of the Orion, but he'd only made it half a dozen paces, before Griff again called out to him. "Oh, and don't get any ideas about flying off in that thing," he said, waving the ship's ID fob at him. He'd evidently removed it from Liberty's belt. "That ship isn't going anywhere without this."

Hudson watched as Griff then crouched down beside Liberty and lifted her chin. Her eyes were still half closed, and she didn't appear to be aware of what was happening. Hudson again had to fight back the urge to charge Griff and tear his throat out. "You have five minutes, rook," said Griff, still holding Liberty's chin between his yellow thumb and forefinger. "It would be a shame if I had to make more of a mess of this pretty little face."

Hudson ran inside the Orion and immediately dashed into the cockpit. Kneeling down in front of the scendar device, he began to dislodge it from its housing. However, as he was doing so, he noticed that the crystal was glowing softly. He frowned, wondering what it might mean, but there was no time to find out. He pulled the device out and hurried back outside, before placing the scendar on the ground at the foot of the ramp.

"The crystal is inside this device," said Hudson, pointing to the scendar. "It's what we used to detect and open the hidden portals."

"Back up, over there" said Griff, motioning Hudson to move away from the ship. Hudson did as he was asked, then Griff cautiously collected the scendar. He peered through the small window in the metal box at the crystal inside and grinned, before walking back beside Liberty.

Suddenly, a deep but distant rumble rippled through the sky around them. Hudson looked up, expecting to see storm clouds, but the sky was perfectly clear. Cutler and Tory also looked up, wearing confused frowns. Only Griff seemed disinterested in the strange and unexpected event. He was too consumed with his victory to be concerned with, or even notice, anything else.

"How does the device work?" Cutler asked, finally speaking up. Hudson was surprised that the mercenary had stayed quiet for so long, especially given how brashly he'd acted on the station.

"The RGF's engineers are more than capable of figuring that out," interrupted Griff, holding a hand up to Cutler to silence him. "We have the crystal and the device, which means we don't need anything more from these two."

Cutler nodded, and Hudson saw the mercenary's fingers tighten around the grip of his weapon. Griff smiled again, baring his yellowed teeth, which contrasted sharply with the rough black fibers of his moustache. Then he said, "Kill the girl first, so he can watch her die."

Hudson jolted forward, but the threat of Cutler's pistol made him think twice. Instead, he turned his panicked eyes to Griff. "We had a deal, Griff!" he roared, paralyzed to the spot. "You said you'd let her go!"

Griff laughed again. It was a loathsome sound that Hudson knew well. It was the same sneering, contemptuous laugh that he'd endured throughout his time as Griff's subordinate. The big difference was that now Griff wasn't just mocking him for sport. This was personal. This was revenge.

"You really are the dumbest rook I ever met," said Griff, as another throaty rumble echoed off the mountains and ridges all around them. Then he turned to Cutler, and added, "Shoot her."

Cutler hesitated, "But what of our agreement..."

"I've changed my mind," Griff interrupted. "I'd much prefer to see Hudson tremble and sob over his dead pet, than make a few extra credits peddling her out in OPW territory."

Cutler nodded, "As you wish." Then he raised the weapon to Liberty's head.

Hudson tried to run at Cutler, but his legs gave way beneath him and he fell forward, hands clawing into the dirt. He tried to cry out, but there was no breath in his lungs. He saw Cutler's finger close around the trigger, but a fraction of a second before the shot was fired, Tory deflected Cutler's aim. The shot rang out, and was lost amongst the growing rumble around them. Hudson could bear it no longer, and his body fell limp. He pressed his forehead to the dust as if in prayer, hoping that the ordeal was over. Liberty was still alive, but for how much longer, he didn't know.

"We made him a deal," Tory snarled, before Cutler could object again. "A deal is a deal. The girl lives."

Griff squared up to Tory, "I make the deals, and I can break the deals," he roared. "The girl dies, because I say she does!"

Griff's oily words had barely escaped his lips, before Tory had lunged at him and slammed a hard, right cross into Griff's face. The RGF officer was caught completely off guard, and staggered back, before dropping down to one knee. Tory advanced again, while Griff was still stunned, grabbing him by the shirt collar, and yanking him towards her.

"You made a deal," she snarled again. "You go back on your word, and *all* deals are off. In that case, I start killing whoever I like, rather than who Cutler tells me to." She shoved him away, and Griff slumped to his back. "And if I'm killing for fun, then I'll start with you."

Griff shot up, face red and furious. His hand went to his weapon, but it wasn't there. Hudson had taken it while he was on the alien station, and it was now stored in one of the ship's lockers. Unarmed and unable to match Tory in hand-to-hand combat, Griff growled and backed down.

"Whatever, I could do with the extra credits anyway," Griff snarled. Then he jabbed a finger at Tory, "But this isn't over between us."

"You honor your agreement and I'll honor mine," Tory hit back. "It's up to you, Inspector." The rumble continued to build, as Tory stood guard over Griff, her hand now clutched around the grip of her six-shooter.

Griff dabbed the side of his face with the back of his hand, all the while glowering at Tory. Then he turned to Cutler, and said, "Let's end this now. Hudson is yours."

The faintest hint of a smile curled Cutler's lips, as he raised the barrel of his weapon towards Hudson. However, before he had chance to pull the trigger, Griff spoke up again. "But I want you to order her to shoot him," he added, pointing his bony finger at Tory.

Cutler scowled at Griff, and Hudson could see a flicker of indecision in his eyes. However, he then lowered his weapon and turned to Tory. For the first time Hudson could see fear behind the formidable female mercenary's eyes. "A deal is a deal, Tory," he told her, coolly. "You said it yourself. Now we shall see if you are also true to your word."

Hudson sensed hostility, bordering on hatred behind Cutler's words. Then another sonorous rumble penetrated the skies, as if the heavens were orchestrating the tension and building it up to a brutal climax. This time Hudson physically felt the roar. It was as if the ridge itself was the scaly back of an enormous dragon that was waking from an eons-long slumber.

Tory Bellona glanced up at the sky, as did the others, but then she glowered back at Cutler. Her expression was harder and icier than Hudson had ever seen before. She then stepped forwards, pushing her partner's weapon down to his side as she passed, and strode up to Hudson.

Hudson rested back on his heels, as Tory peered down at him. The mercenary had saved him – and Liberty – several times before, but this time he could see no escape.

Tory drew her single action revolver, and cocked it. Though at the same time, Hudson saw her draw a second weapon with her left hand, and raise it next to the six-shooter. It was done so swiftly, that it was almost seamless. And, with her back to Griff and Cutler, Hudson doubted that the others would have even seen it.

A shot rang out, near deafening due to Tory's close proximity, and Hudson felt the stab of pain. His strength was instantly sapped from his body, and he fell backwards, unable to move. He saw Tory's face above him, smoke from the barrel of her six-shooter obscuring her features. A dark cloud then swept across her, shrouding her in a veil of darkness. Hudson thought he was dying, but then the source of the dark shadow revealed itself, as an alien shuttle swooped in over the ridge.

Hudson heard terrified cries of 'run!', and the sounds of weapons being fired, but they were distant and wooly in his ears. The dark shape above him began to merge with the darkness consuming his vision. Soon, the alien ship had gone. Tory had gone. And then the alien world itself dissolved to nothing.

CHAPTER 15

Hudson woke, face down in the gravelly dirt on top of the ridge. He pushed himself up, spitting grit from his mouth, and sat upright against the side of a smooth, flat rock. He still felt dizzy and disorientated, and was uncertain of where he was, and why he was there. Everything was a chaotic jumble. All he knew for certain was that there was a stinging pain in his neck, and his head felt like it had been used as a punching bag.

Hudson tried to stand, but dizziness and nausea nearly overwhelmed him. He managed to steady himself against the cool rock, but his vision was still foggy. He squeezed his eyes shut and slapped the side of his face with the palm of his hand, trying to literally knock some sense into himself. However, all he succeeded in doing was brushing more dirt off his numb-feeling face.

"Self-administered physical harm will not improve your situation," a voice said.

Hudson spun around, looking for the source of the words, but he was still struggling to focus. Then he saw a blur approaching. He reached for his pistol, before remembering that Griff had made him toss it away. Instead, he raised his guard, and squared off against the blur as best he could, given his bleary condition.

"In a contest of physical combat, you would not fare well against me," the voice said, though it didn't sound like a threat. And, oddly, the voice sounded different to the first one he'd heard. He wondered if there was more than one person, but he could still see only a single shape.

"Who are you?" demanded Hudson, blinking rapidly in an effort to force his eyes to focus.

"Your companion called me Morphus," the voice said, though it sounded different again. He had initially discerned two distinct male voices, but now it was clearly a woman. "In the absence of a more suitable designation, I have adopted this moniker."

"Morphus?" repeated Hudson, wracking his battered brain for where he'd heard the name before. Then he remembered, "Wait, you mean you're the alien we found on Bach Two?"

"Correct," said Morphus. "But, from my perspective, you are the alien. In actuality, we are merely two unique intelligences, neither one more alien than the other."

"Well, you're just a uniquely intelligent blur to me at the moment," said Hudson, dropping to one knee. His body lacked even the strength to stand. The fog in his head was lifting steadily, and his mind finally caught up with recent events. *Oh no! Liberty!* he thought, as he remembered what had happened. Filled with dread, he sprang up, boosted by a sudden rush of adrenalin. "Can you tell me what happened to Liberty?!"

Suddenly, Hudson felt a hand close around his arm, followed by a sharp prick in his neck. Almost immediately, his vision cleared, and his aches and pains seemed to melt away. He also felt calm. The urgent need to find out about Liberty remained, as did his deep-rooted concern for her, but the raw, primal emotions had been subdued somehow.

He looked up at the entity that was holding his arm. It had apparently changed form again, and now appeared as a man, though wearing another new face, not the one he remembered. Its clothing was a replica of the same items Hudson was wearing, except as before it was like the clothing was seamlessly sewn onto his body.

"The chemical substances I just injected into your bloodstream will have mitigated the extreme emotional distress you were experiencing," said Morphus, calmly.

"Mitigated is one way of putting it," said Hudson, feeling completely centered and in control. The contrast was stark compared to how he'd felt only seconds earlier. Wasting no time, he quickly scouted the area for signs of Liberty, Griff and the others. He saw his pistol lying in the dirt, and replaced it in his shoulder holster, before moving to the far side of the ridge. There, resting on another clearing about a hundred meters lower down, was the alien shuttle belonging to Morphus. Then he remembered seeing a shape flying overhead, just after Tory had shot him. The shape must have been Morphus' ship, he realized. *Talk about arriving in the nick of time...* Hudson thought to himself.

Hudson glanced back at the alien entity, noticing that Morphus had joined him on the edge of the ridge. "Do you know what happened to Liberty?" Hudson asked again. Then his head hung low, "Do you know if they... killed her?"

"No, the corporeal entity you call Logan Griff took her with him on his vessel," said Morphus. "Based on the communications I monitored, my understanding is that he intends to trade the Liberty Devan entity in return for a denomination of currency." Then Morphus looked at Hudson, his expression imitating human quizzicality precisely. "Is it normal in your society to trade corporeals in this way?"

Hudson sighed, "In some places, I'm afraid so." Then he had a thought, "Wait, if you monitored their communications, do you know where Griff was taking her? I mean the planet or the station where he intends to sell her?"

Morphus seemed to think for a moment, and then answered, "Yes. The facility is called New Providence. It is located within the grouping of distinct planetary bodies that you identify as the Union of Outer Portal Worlds."

Hudson shook his head, "Shit, I know about that place," he said, before letting out another exasperated sigh. As a courier runner, he'd tried to avoid the OPW territories as much as possible, though sometimes the danger bounties were just too tempting to ignore. New Providence was a cesspit of the worst kinds of lowlifes in the galaxy. And although there was a functioning government, the station was actually controlled by one of the largest criminal gangs, simply known as The Council.

Over decades, the influence of these underworld organizations had largely been eradicated from the inner portal worlds, which were tightly controlled by the CET and MP. However, the Outer Portal Worlds were a fractured mess of corruption, crime and vice. Recovering Liberty from that nest of vipers without getting killed or robbed would be more difficult than drinking Ma under the table. Not that he had a choice – he had to try.

Thankfully, the heady concoction of substances Morphus had pumped into him had given Hudson the advantage of a clear head. Rushing off unprepared to New Providence would not help his chances of finding Liberty. And since Morphus was proving to be a fount of knowledge, he first wanted to get some more answers from the mysterious alien. And that included how and why it had arrived just in time to save his life.

Hudson again turned to face Morphus, but recoiled in shock, as the being had shifted into the form of a woman. "Can you just pick one face and stick to it?" complained Hudson, struggling to keep up with the alien's numerous identities.

"I have yet to select a single form," Morphus replied. "Your species offers so many variant options, it is challenging to fix on one."

Hudson tried to ignore the distracting effect of the being's constant shape-shifting, and thought back to the first time he'd encountered Morphus. The being had then appeared in the living space of the Orion, and talked of something called Goliath. The memory sent a chill down his spine.

"The last time we met, you talked about Earth being wiped out," Hudson began, getting straight to the point. "No offence, but I was too freaked out by you at the time to take any of it in. For some reason, I feel much more in control now. Don't ask me why."

"There would be no benefit to me asking you why, since you do not have the answer," replied Morphus, mimicking a look of human confusion very well. "However, the reason for your calmer condition now is that I injected reuptake inhibitors into your bloodstream," Morphus continued.

"I don't know what the hell that means," laughed Hudson, starting to feel lost and overwhelmed. He glanced at the alien shuttle, and then to where he'd last seen Liberty, barely conscious and bleeding, and shook his head. "I don't know what any of this means. We arrive here and the alien space station just 'turns on', before blowing up. Then on this planet, I find another alien ship that rises out of the rocks, like a phoenix from the ashes. Then Liberty is taken from me, I almost get killed, and you appear at the last second to save my ass. I feel like I'm in way over my head."

"I did not save you," interrupted Morphus.

Hudson frowned and turned to face the being, "But I saw your ship fly overhead and scare Cutler and Griff away," Hudson was grateful that Morphus had retained its current form for more than a couple of minutes. "If you didn't come here to save me, then why did you?"

Morphus appeared to not understand Hudson's frantic questions. The entity seemed to have no problem with responding to direct inquiries, where there was only a definitive answer, such as asking for the result of a mathematical problem.

However, more nuanced questions – or perhaps more 'human' questions – that required Morphus to provide its own interpretation of events appeared to be more challenging for the alien.

"I will answer as succinctly as your corporeal spoken language allows," said Morphus. "But before I do, I must know where the crystal is."

Hudson frowned, "The crystal? It was taken, by Logan Griff."

Morphus also frowned, copying Hudson's own expression exactly. "That is unfortunate."

"Why?" asked Hudson, "What's so important about that damn crystal?"

"The crystal is the only hope of defeating Goliath," Morphus answered. "To answer your earlier question, that is why I am here."

Hudson was about to dig deeper into the vague answer Morphus had given. However, the alien entity seemed to sense Hudson's intentions, and quickly headed him off.

"I will explain in more detail later, but right now, all you need to know is that if Goliath returns, it will destroy all sentient life. Not only all of the sentient corporeals on the planet you call Earth, but the corporeal colonies on your moon, the planet you call Mars, and all of the other worlds your species now inhabits."

There was a pause, as Morphus allowed Hudson to process what he had just been told. "It is imperative that we recover the crystal. Everything hinges on this."

"We?" said Hudson, recoiling slightly. "When did this become 'we'?"

"I am the last Revocater," said Morphus, and he gestured to the alien wreck on the horizon. "The others like me all fell to Goliath. I cannot defeat the great ship alone. I require assistance."

"The others?" queried Hudson, but then he looked at the fractured wreck, and he suddenly understood. "The alien hulks – they were these Revocaters you talk about?" Morphus simply nodded. "And Goliath destroyed them all?" Hudson continued, realizing that his voice had risen half an octave. Morphus nodded again, and then Hudson laughed, nervously. He was finally beginning to understand something of the background to this strange, shape-shifting being.

"Hell, Morphus, I'm just a washed-up old flyer in the midst of a mid-life crisis, with a ship the size of a flea compared to these Revocaters. I'm sorry, but I don't know what I can possibly do to help." Then the image of Griff punching Liberty invaded his thoughts again, and he closed his eyes. "Besides, all I can think about right now is finding Liberty."

"I will assist you in recovering your corporeal ally," said Morphus. "If you will help me to find and recover the crystal, and defeat Goliath."

"I appreciate the offer of help," said Hudson, his eyes widening, "but you'd be better off going to the governments of the CET or the MP. They have resources and soldiers and warships that can fight this Goliath."

"Your armadas and soldiers are no match for the great ship," replied Morphus, flatly. "And based on the data I have gathered so far, your governments cannot be trusted. However, according to my assessments you, Hudson Powell, can be."

Hudson laughed again and shook his head, before peering out at the wreck. "Thanks for the vote of confidence," he said. Then he considered how it would be nigh on impossible for him to find Liberty on New Providence by himself. "And I can't deny that I could use the help," he added, thinking out loud. Then he turned back at Morphus, and made a decision. He hoped it was a good one. "If you help me rescue Liberty, then I promise I'll do whatever I can to help you defeat Goliath. But, in all honesty, I think you've drawn the short straw."

Morphus appeared confused again, and started to look around the ridge, "I do not see any straw, long or short?"

Hudson smiled, "Never mind. So, what happens now?"

Morphus met Hudson's eyes again. "Follow me into orbit, and we can begin the search for your corporeal ally."

Hudson nodded, and then took a step towards the Orion, before he noticed something crushed into the sandy soil at his feet. He picked the object up and it immediately fell apart in his hands, before he realized what it was. "Shit, I'm afraid I'm not going anywhere soon," he said, causing Morphus to arrest his descent towards his own ship, and walk back up onto the ridge. "This is the Orion's ID fob. Without this, I can't start her up. Not without an engineering genius to hotwire it, and she's on her way to New Providence station."

Morphus reached out and took the remains of the ID fob, turning it over in its hands. Suddenly, Morphus changed form, its entire body becoming glacially smooth and featureless, and turning a fine golden color like champagne. It looked like a sculpture of a woman, formed entirely from liquid metal. Hudson was completely awed by the spectacle, which only lasted a few seconds, before the humanoid form of Morphus returned. This time, it was back to looking like a man.

Morphus threw down the crushed fob, then reached out and grabbed Hudson's wrist. He felt his skin become warmer, and his entire arm began to tingle, but he was still too stunned to resist. Before he knew what had happened, Morphus had released his hand again. Hudson then peered down and saw a light gold patch about the size of a postage stamp in the center of his wrist. He touched it, and though it felt metallic, there was no discomfort.

"What the hell is this?" he said, after his senses caught up enough that he could speak.

"I have grafted the technology contained within your ID fob directly into your skeletal structure," said Morphus, in an entirely matter-of-fact manner. "You can now operate your vessel."

"Thanks," said Hudson, staring at the patch, wide-eyed. "Though, the next time you plan on grafting stuff to my skeleton, could you maybe give me a heads-up first?" He felt like he'd just been partly assimilated into a cyborg.

Morphus took a moment to consider this, but then seemed to understand. "As you wish, Hudson Powell entity. I will see you in orbit."

Then Morphus turned again, but after a few paces Hudson called out to it to stop. He recalled something Morphus had said earlier that he still hadn't got an answer to. For some reason the question had wormed its way back to the front of his mind again.

"Hey, before, when you said you didn't save me," Hudson began. "What exactly did you mean by that?"

Morphus took a moment to process the question, before responding. "I was pursuing the signal generated by the active crystal. As you presumed, its unique signature is responsible for activating the space station, and also the other vessel you encountered. But my arrival at the moment of your peril was purely coincidental."

"Then how come I'm still alive?" Hudson replied. "Tory Bellona, the female mercenary who was here, shot me at point blank range. There's no way I could have survived that."

Morphus held out his hand, palm upwards, and suddenly it became smooth and almost liquid. An object appeared in the center, as if it had bubbled up to the surface, like flotsam in the sea, before the hand returned to normal again. Hudson stepped closer and then took the object between his finger and thumb.

"This is a tranquillizer dart," said Hudson, now more befuddled than ever. "Where the hell did you get this?"

"The corporeal you referred to as Tory Bellona shot this into your neck, while simultaneously discharging a firearm into the ground behind you," answered Morphus. The entity then turned back towards his ship. "You have the Tory Bellona entity to thank for your survival, not I."

CHAPTER 16

Hudson strapped himself into the pilot's seat, and activated the pre-flight systems. The navigation scanner immediately bleeped, and displayed a unique star-shaped chevron in close proximity to the Orion. Hudson arched his neck to peer out through the cockpit glass, and then saw Morphus' vessel hovering nearby. He remembered that Liberty had earlier calibrated the scanner to pick up the alien ship. However, whereas Morphus had previously been attempting to remain hidden, now it was operating in plain sight.

"Well, my wingman or woman is here," said Hudson, getting everything set for take-off. "Only question is, how the hell do I start the engines?" He looked at the ID scanner port, where normally he would attach the ID fob, then tentatively waved his wrist in front of it. The metallic patch that Morphus had grafted to his skeleton glowed brightly, causing him to jolt back and shake his arm, as if trying to extinguish a fire. Then he heard the engines spark into life, and all the other ship's systems began to spool up too. "Well, I'll be damned, it actually worked," said Hudson, staring at his wrist. It was still glowing softly, but he felt no pain or discomfort at all.

Lowering his arm again, he checked his boards and saw that all systems showed green. Hudson smiled, realizing that Liberty had done her usual stellar job of looking after the ship. He glanced over to the empty second seat and his smile fell away. Her absence was as stark as a gaping hole in the hull. He'd spent half his life flying solo from one portal world to another, but now the thought of being on his own terrified and saddened him in equal measure.

Hudson tried to park these darker thoughts, and grabbed the controls, lifting the Orion off the ridge and into the now dusky sky. The black shape of Morphus' ship edged in front of him, and he slotted in behind as the alien vessel climbed higher. Compared to the Orion, Morphus' ship had a far more organic appearance. It looked like it had been sculpted from an inky black clay, rather than hammered together from a bunch of metal panels and frames. It was elegant, in an unearthly way. Even the manner in which it moved through the sky seemed to defy logic, and physics.

The orange sky melted away to darkness as the two ships passed out of the atmosphere and into space. It wasn't long before the remains of the alien space station, still burning brightly, became visible. Flashes occasionally popped off all along its surface, but then Hudson realized that there were other flashes ahead too, and these weren't coming from the space station. Sensing something was wrong, Hudson hurriedly checked the navigation scanner to determine what other vessels were still in the system.

The scan updated and Hudson noticed that only a couple of the contacts were relic hunter ships. However, a small fleet of MP military vessels had since arrived to secure the portal. Hudson noted that the large cruiser that had joined the initial expedition was still there, but it had been joined by five smaller vessels – two destroyers and three gunboats. Oddly, they were not in formation, Hudson realized, nor were they guarding the portal location. Then he spotted another chevron on the scanner. It was red, like the strange contact the scendar device had detected, far out towards the galactic center. However, with the scendar gone, the navigation scanner was no longer detecting anything beyond the limited range of its human-designed sensors. Whatever this new contact was, it was close by, Hudson realized. And it was also moving fast.

An incoming audio communication pulled Hudson's attention away from the scanner. He scowled at the display, which was unable to determine the origin of the signal, but he answered it anyway.

"This is Morphus," a female voice said. "Does your vessel carry weapons?"

"Yes," said Hudson, getting a sinking feeling that he was going to need them.

"Then activate your defensive systems and stay close to my ship," replied Morphus. "The vessel you discovered on the surface is here. In your words, the best description is that it is a seed drone. It has been inactive for millennia, but its memory core has been rejuvenated, and it is now continuing its directive."

"And what directive is that?" Hudson asked, knowing he probably wouldn't like the answer.

"To exterminate sentient organic life," Morphus answered, with an almost chilling aloofness. "Then it will search for Goliath and rejoin it. It must be destroyed."

"Roger that," said Hudson, quickly arming the weapons systems. He heard the comforting whirs and thuds as gears wound the turret and cannon out from their hidden stows. Targeting reticules appeared on the cockpit glass. Hudson set the turret to automatic tracking, but configured the nose cannon for manual control. "Okay, weapons are hot," Hudson said into the mic. "Assuming they'll do any good against this seed drone you mentioned."

"Most likely not," replied Morphus.

Hudson laughed, "You really have to work on your motivational techniques," he said, but the radio silence he received in return told him that his joke had gone over the alien's head. "What is that thing, anyway?" he added, choosing a question he knew that Morphus would be able to answer.

"They were once a part of Goliath," Morphus answered. "At one time they helped to bring life to empty worlds. Now, they are the great ship's foot soldiers, and they only seek to destroy."

Hudson shook his head, "Maybe one day, you'll have some good news to share."

"Maybe," said Morphus, "but not this day. Stay close."

The channel remained open, and Hudson let out another long breath, while gripping the controls tightly. More flashes popped off ahead and Hudson saw one of the MP gunboats explode into flames. Five MP vessels remained, but as he approached the combat zone, he could now see the burning remains of two other destroyers that had already been obliterated.

Hudson stayed on Morphus' tail, until both had approached to within visual range of the other vessels. His panel bleeped another incoming message, but this time it was from the lead MP

Cruiser. Tentatively, Hudson opened the channel and put the message through.

"This is Admiral Shelby to relic hunter vessel VCX-110, M7070-Orion," the message began, "You are ordered to steer clear of the portal. We are engaged with hostile forces. I repeat steer clear of the portal. This is your only warning."

Hudson then noticed that the two MP destroyers had broken off, and were heading towards him. "What the hell are they attacking me for?" he said out loud. Then he felt his skin go cold as he realized who the MP destroyers were actually gunning for. "Shit, they're after Morphus, not me!"

Hudson saw cannons flash ahead and he thrusted hard to stern to avoid the incoming fire, while Morphus broke hard to port. He quickly opened a channel back to the lead cruiser. "This is relic hunter Orion to Admiral Shelby. Do not fire on the second alien vessel – it is not hostile. Repeat, it is not hostile, do not fire!"

"Orion, clear this channel and withdraw, or you will also be considered a hostile. I will not warn you again." The channel then clicked off, as abruptly as the Admiral had spoken.

"Damn stuck-up, arrogant Martian assholes!" Hudson yelled into the microphone, before weaving the Orion between the two destroyers. He saw the red chevron closing in, and then checked the position of the portal. He adjusted his course and tightened the straps of his seat. All his instincts told him to turn tail and fly away in the opposite direction as fast as he could. However, if he was going to find Liberty, then he had no choice but to get out of the system as quickly as possible. And that meant he had no choice but to fly directly into the heart of the battle, and make a run for it.

CHAPTER 17

A gunboat surged out in front of the Orion, and Hudson saw turrets light up as it opened fire. Tracer rounds flashed above him as he pushed the Orion lower, narrowly evading the shots.

"I'm not a hostile, you Martian morons!" Hudson yelled, shaking his fist at the gunboat. Suddenly, he saw the vessel Morphus had called a seed drone soar above him, like a shining black arrowhead. He watched, mouth agape, as the vessel raced towards the MP gunboat, on a collision course. The gunboat opened fire, striking the alien vessel cleanly, but the only effect was to deflect it off course. The arrow-shaped ship shot past the gunboat, but then spun around in a maneuver that defied physics. The MP ship tried desperately to turn its weapons on the vessel again, but it was too late. The seed drone accelerated, slicing through the center of the gunboat like an axe blade through rotten wood. Seconds later, the MP vessel was consumed in fire and blown apart.

Hudson tried to put the image out of his mind, and spun the Orion around to line-up with the portal. He then pushed the thrusters hard and began to accelerate towards his target. However, Admiral Shelby's cruiser still loomed in front of the opening, like a goalkeeper. His eyes flashed to the navigation scanner to check the positions of the other ships, and he adjusted course to avoid being caught in a crossfire. Then an intense flash of light filled the cockpit, forcing him to shield his eyes. When the glow subsided, he saw that the alien vessel had now punched through the hull of an MP Destroyer. However, this latest attack had placed the seed drone directly in Hudson's line of fire.

Hudson locked on to the alien combatant, seeing an opportunity to get into the fight. His heart was racing and his mouth was dry as he squeezed the trigger, sending a volley of rounds snaking off into space. He saw the rounds land on target and then punched the air. Yet the alien seed drone merely continued onward, showing no signs of damage.

"What the hell?!" Hudson called out, but then his pounding heart almost stopped, as the alien ship turned to bear down on him. Hudson veered away and rammed the throttle control forward, but the Orion lacked the alien vessel's seemingly impossible maneuverability.

Suddenly, he saw Morphus' shuttle blast past the cockpit glass, and fire focused bolts of energy at the seed drone. The arrow-shaped ship evaded and then the two alien vessels broke off, weaving and turning with unfeasible agility. It was like they were world war one fighter aces, dogfighting in the skies above Europe. There was simply no chance any of the MP vessels could compete with them in combat. It was a mismatch on a laughable scale.

Flashes of energy tore across space as the two alien vessels continued their intricate ballet, until Morphus scored a hit. The alien seed drone then spiraled out of control, sparking like a firework.

Hudson punched the air again, but then watched in horror as the seed drone collided with an MP Gunboat. The two ships exploded with an almost thermonuclear violence, sending burning debris in all directions. Hudson narrowly evaded one of the flaming hunks of metal, and resumed course for the portal. Cannon shells and tracer rounds were still criss-crossing space all around him, as the remaining MP forces tried in vain to scores hits on Morphus' maneuverable alien vessel. It was like trying to walk through the center of no-man's land during the Battle of the Somme.

He'd barely made it five hundred meters, before alarms shrieked inside the cockpit and he felt the ship shudder. Hudson took emergency evasive action again, while quickly scanning his array of screens for a damage readout. Red lights showed across a dozen systems. He didn't know how bad it was, and he had no time to find out. More than ever, he wished he had Liberty in the second seat. Without her expertise and reassuring presence, he felt vulnerable, exposed, and utterly alone.

"Come on, move out of the way, you Martian hunk of crap!" Hudson called out to the cruiser, as if yelling would make Admiral Shelby retreat. Then he saw Morphus again. The alien ship buzzed past the cruiser at such frighteningly close range that he hoped Admiral Shelby didn't have a weak heart. The cruiser took the bait, and reoriented itself so that it could bring the full measure of its formidable weapons to bear on the alien.

Hudson saw the cruiser's cannons light up as it engaged Morphus. He took a deep breath and flexed his fingers, which had become drained of blood from gripping the controls tightly. *This is my chance...* he told himself. *It's now or never...* He lined up the nose of the Orion with the portal, and pulsed the main engines, accelerating him towards it at what would ordinarily be a dangerously unsafe velocity. However, with Admiral Shelby's ship momentarily out of position, it was his only chance.

The MP Cruiser launched another full broadside at Morphus' ship, and Hudson saw it take a hit. The energy of the shell striking its hull knocked Morphus into a spin, like a pool ball striking another. Yet, there were no flames, or any evidence of damage at all. *Tough little ship...* thought Hudson. In contrast, a single cannon shell from an MP cruiser would have annihilated the Orion in one hit.

Hudson glanced at his instruments, checking the distance to the portal. He then made a snap judgement call, spinning the engine pods one hundred and eighty degrees and decelerating rapidly. The g-forces almost caused him to black out, but he remained alert enough to fire the thrusters to line-up with the portal. It was a gutsy move that could have easily seen him overshoot, but fortune favored him this time.

Suddenly, he felt a series of impacts hammer the hull, and more red lights started to fill up the damage control panel. He could already feel atmosphere leaking out of the cockpit, but emergency seals fell into place to stop the cold vacuum of space from consuming him.

Hudson pushed the throttle control forward, but the thrusters didn't respond. "Come on, don't let me down now!" Hudson cried, trying to talk the ship into responding.

With time running out, he rapidly switched to secondary backups, but a power surge overloaded the panel. He slammed his fists on the flight deck and looked out of the cockpit glass at the portal. It was less than one hundred meters away, but without propulsion, it might as well have been a light year. His thoughts turned to Liberty, and how Griff intended to sell her off as if he was auctioning a relic, and he gritted his teeth. He wasn't giving up. Not now. Not ever.

Hudson unclipped his harness and scrambled over to the second seat, throwing open the service panel. Fuses crackled and sparked, as he reached inside, flicking out the damaged components, which fizzed on the deck like firecrackers. With the Orion now listing in space, it had slowly spun on its axis. Glancing up, Hudson saw the MP Cruiser slowly arcing back towards the portal. Admiral Shelby clearly had no intention of letting Hudson escape.

Working faster, he replaced the damaged fuses and slammed the panel shut, before running back to the pilot's chair. "Come on, please!" Hudson pleaded, flicking the initiator to restart the thruster systems. He closed his eyes and waited. Agonizing seconds passed, and the thruster controls finally reinitiated. He had power, but the MP Cruiser was almost on top of him.

Then out of the darkness he saw Morphus approaching. The alien ship lashed the cruiser across the back with red bolts of energy, picking off its turrets with pinpoint accuracy, before breaking away and powering towards the portal.

Hudson slammed the thruster lever forward, as the cruiser completed its turn, bringing its powerful forward cannons in line with the Orion.

151

One shot would be all that was needed to reduce him to atoms.

Hudson held his breath, expecting to be consumed by fire and fury. However, instead, the cockpit was filled with spiraling purple light, as the Orion entered the portal, and jumped.

CHAPTER 18

The Orion emerged from the portal in an uncontrolled spin, toppling slowly, end-over-end, towards the tiny moon of Phobos. The already damaged drive systems immediately shut down. Hudson knew this was a normal side-effect of portal transitions, but without Liberty, it could take him up to twenty minutes to restart them. And in all that time, the Orion was a sitting duck.

Hudson peered down at the damage control panel and saw that the Orion was in bad shape. Worse still, the cockpit had been sealed off from the rest of the ship, due to a pressure differential. Hudson knew this indicated a hull breach somewhere in the cockpit. In order to restart the drive systems Hudson had to reach engineering, but until he could plug the leak, he was stuck where he was.

Hudson unclipped his harness and rushed to the disaster pod at the rear of the cockpit. Inside was the gear he would need to survive in the event the ship lost pressure completely. He removed the lightweight space suit and pulled it on over the top of his relic hunting gear. Combined with the compact helmet, it could be pressurized in the event that the cockpit was exposed to the vacuum of space. However, the prospect of having to abandon ship, and voluntarily venture into the void in the hope of rescue, filled Hudson with dread.

He left the helmet on the pilot's seat, and began to search for the source of the leak. For the moment, the cockpit still had air and heat. His suit also had an emergency oxygen supply, but he intended to keep this as a last resort, in case he was stranded for hours, awaiting rescue.

Searching methodically from one side of the cockpit to the next, he quickly found the breach. The cockpit glass had been cracked on the starboard side, and it looked like there was a minor puncture to the hull below it. The emergency seal for the hull breach was secure, but he could see now that the crack to the cockpit glass was slowly spreading.

Hudson had seen enough dinged windscreens to know that in the event of damage to the cockpit glass, a protective shutter should fall. That this safeguarding measure had failed meant his survival now called for more desperate measures.

He ran back to the disaster pod, and sifted through the contents, until he found the resin applicator. This was designed to temporarily seal cracks in the cockpit glass, until repairs could be made. If he was lucky, and the crack didn't widen much further, it would maintain the integrity of the cockpit long enough for Hudson to re-pressurize, get to engineering and then limp to a repair facility.

Quickly returning to the damaged window, Hudson was then distracted by a bright purple flash. "Shit, that's another ship coming through the portal..." Hudson realized, finding comfort in speaking the words out loud. Without the main drive systems running, the cockpit was deathly quiet, and hearing his own voice somehow made it feel less intimidating. Even so, with the cabin temperature falling by the minute, Hudson was struggling to fight the fear that was vying to overwhelm him.

He dashed back to the pilot's seat and tried to use the Orion's impaired thrusters to correct the ship's spin. Whoever had just transitioned through the portal would also suffer a main drive failure, but their weapon systems would still be online. And with the Orion listing helplessly in space, even thrusters would be enough to catch up with him. Chances were that it was the MP cruiser, Hudson reasoned, but even if it was an ignoble relic hunter looking for an easy target, he was in big trouble.

Hudson managed to stabilize the ship and orient it towards the portal. The question of who had just arrived was then answered. Looming large above him was the powerful MP Cruiser, commanded by Admiral Shelby.

"Shit, I'd almost prefer it to be another hunter..." mused Hudson, before rushing back to the damaged glass to apply the resin. The arrival of the cruiser added an even greater sense of urgency to what was already a desperate situation. Hudson managed to cover about fifty percent of the crack, when the communications systems chimed an incoming message. Hudson didn't need to look at the panel to know who it was. He reached across to the console on the second seat and flipped open the channel.

Admiral Shelby's haughty, condescending tones immediately filled the cockpit. "Relic hunter Orion, this is Admiral Shelby," she began, sounding slightly flustered. This was an emotional state that Hudson did not typically associate with Martians, and especially not those from the MP military. "You are under arrest for disobeying a direct command from an MP military vessel, while in Martian Protectorate territory," Shelby continued. "Stand down and prepare to be boarded."

Hudson finished applying the resin and then dropped down into the second seat. If there was one thing that could distract his fragile mind from an impending, icy death in space, it was a snooty MP Admiral talking to him like a seven-year old.

"Admiral Shelby, this is Captain Hudson Powell of the Orion," Hudson began, steeling himself for a fight. "I may not be an expert in the regulations surrounding new portal worlds," he continued, unable to hide his disdain, "but I'm pretty sure that any system is considered neutral territory until the MP government makes an official declaration."

"Captain, let's not mince words," Shelby replied, after a brief delay. For an MP officer, Shelby was surprisingly swift to dispense with formalities. "You were spotted in formation with a hostile alien force. You have questions to answer, and I intend to get them. Remain where you are. If I must, I will further disable your already stricken vessel. It would be better – and safer – for you, if you simply complied with my directives."

Hudson shook his head. Shelby's mind seemed set, but despite her threats, he wasn't going to be pushed around. "I don't know what you're talking about, Admiral," Hudson hit back, forgetting for a moment just how much danger he was still in. "I was just running like hell to get away from whatever those alien ships were. Maybe you should go back there and find out, rather than harassing an honest relic hunter like me."

Hudson heard Admiral Shelby laugh derisively, presumably at the notion of an 'honest relic hunter'. Then she delivered a succinct reply. "You claimed it was not hostile. You clearly know more than you are letting on, and I intend to find out what. Shelby out."

The channel to the MP Cruiser clicked off, and Hudson aimed an impassioned 'up yours' gesture at the console, before checking the cabin pressure. It had stabilized, and was steadily starting to creep upwards. However, it would still be a few minutes before the automatic seal on the cockpit door would release. And then he would still have to re-start the Orion's drive systems before Shelby's engineers could restore power to the cruiser.

Hudson had done more re-starts than he cared to count, and he was pretty good at them. Even so, his record was just over twenty-two minutes – well short of Liberty's best. He knew that the big cruisers, such as the one threatening him now, typically took longer. However, though he hated the self-satisfied arrogance of the Martian military, their confidence was not unjustified. Ultimately, which ship got their engines started first would be a close-run contest.

Hudson rested back in the seat and closed his eyes. Until the cockpit fully pressurized again, who could restart the drive systems faster was a moot point, because at the moment he was going nowhere.

The silence and calm in the cockpit were almost meditative, and Hudson felt himself starting to doze off. Suddenly, alarms shrieked out and the abrupt jolt of shock nearly knocked him out of his seat. His heart thudded in his chest, as he saw another damage warning light flash up. Then he checked the pressure and saw it was dropping again, this time rapidly. Looking over to the cracked window, he saw to his horror that the resin had failed. The crack was snaking wider, and there was nothing he could do about it.

"Shit!" he cried out, scrambling to reach the pilot's chair, where he'd left his helmet. However, he was already struggling to breathe and the sudden drop in oxygen level was causing him to become disorientated too. Hudson dropped to his knees in front of the pilot's chair and grasped the helmet, before clumsily pulling it on. Struggling with the locking mechanism, he finally managed to secure the helmet over the collar. He waited, but there was no hiss of oxygen.

"What the hell?" Hudson cried out, feeling the primal terror grip him fully. He stared over at the disaster pod, and realized that in his haste to put on the suit, he hadn't connected the oxygen reservoirs. With his already oxygen-starved breaths becoming ever more frantic and labored, Hudson clambered across the deck towards the pod. But dizziness caused him to stumble and fall.

I'm sorry, Liberty... Hudson thought, as he used what little strength he had left to roll onto his back.

He knew he was finished. *I really screwed this one up. I'm sorry...*

Hudson stared out at the MP cruiser, still visible through the cockpit glass. He wondered whether Shelby would try to save him, or if the Admiral would be content to let him suffocate and die. However, even if she did attempt a rescue, there was little chance that a shuttle could reach him before it was too late.

It was fun while it lasted, thought Hudson, managing a feeble smile. If he was going to die, he was damned if his final thoughts would be as dark as the space enveloping him. *I finally got to do something I care about.* Then thoughts of Liberty pushed their way back into his mind. *At least she's still alive,* he told himself, still fighting the darkness. *She has a chance. If anyone can survive out in New Providence, it's her.*

He continued to stare out into space while his breathing became shallower. Then the cruiser suddenly blinked out of view, as a black shadow swooped in between it and the Orion. He heard the communications system crackle on.

"Hudson Powell entity, this is Morphus. Standby." If Hudson had any air left in his lungs, he would have laughed out loud. Then he felt a hard thud against the hull, and the starlight vanished, as if the cockpit had just been shrouded in an enormous blanket. "Don't worry, Hudson Powell entity," he heard Morphus add. "I am coming."

CHAPTER 19

There had only been a few occasions during Hudson's career as a freelance pilot that he'd needed rescuing. And while floating helplessly in space was never a pleasant experience, he'd not felt truly in danger on those occasions. Certainly nothing on the scale of the near-death experience he'd just lived through.

During his previous interstellar breakdowns, the life support systems had never failed, and he'd never been all that far from a helpful tug ship or a welcoming repair dock. He'd always felt safe piloting space ships, despite the narrow skin of metal and glass that separated him from the cold vacuum of space. However, now Hudson truly understood how dangerous space travel really was. He'd been lucky to make it past Admiral Shelby's blockade alive. And had it not been for the truly extraordinary manner of his rescue, he would have surely perished on the Martian-side of the portal. Instead, he was alive and safe; at least for now.

Morphus had descended on the Orion literally in the nick of time. However, unlike his chance intervention on the planet's surface, this time Morphus had come to Hudson's aid intentionally. The alien entity's vessel, unlike all human-built craft, had not suffered any adverse effects from the portal transition. And, like Morphus itself, the ship had seemed to possess an ability to transform its shape. It was a far cry from the near fluid-like transitions that Morphus went through when switching between its many identities. Yet while it was a more mechanical process, the alien ship was still flexible and graceful enough to adapt to the shape of the Orion's hull, and seal the breach.

Not only this, but Morphus had then rapidly towed the Orion away from the portal, before Shelby's cruiser had regained power. And, thanks to the Orion's drive systems being offline, and Morphus shielding his energy signature, Shelby had been unable to track them. As such, their current location, hovering just above the surface inside the Stickney Crater on Phobos, was known to no-one but them.

Even more remarkable than the nature of Hudson's rescue, was the fact that Morphus had also managed to repair the Orion. It had taken just over a day, all in, and Hudson had slept for fully half of this time. However, when he woke up, he couldn't believe the transformation. It would have taken a week in a repair dock to achieve what Morphus had done, alone and in the vacuum of space. Though as Hudson ran his hand along the newly-repaired cockpit glass, he realized that Morphus hadn't just repaired the Orion – the entity had augmented it too. The glass was no longer glass at all, but some unique transparent alien compound that felt oddly warm to the touch. And all around the ship, he could see adaptations and reinforcements to the structural skeleton of the Orion, all made from the unique alien metal.

"Your vessel is now operating at ninety-eight-point-seven percent efficiency," said Morphus, causing Hudson to jolt around in surprise.

"You scared the crap out of me," said Hudson, pressing a hand to his chest. Then the puzzled look on Morphus' face – currently that of a thirty-something female – made him feel the need to clarify. "Not literally, in case that's why you're making that face. It's just an expression that means you took me by surprise."

"I apologize for causing your sudden release of glutamate and adrenalin," said Morphus. This caused Hudson to raise a quizzical eyebrow, but Morphus went on, apparently unaware of Hudson's confusion. "Are you satisfied with the repairs?"

"Satisfied?" Hudson laughed. Then he spun around, looking at the cockpit of the VCX-110, which was like new. "It would have bankrupted me to get these repairs done at Deimos. I honestly don't know how to thank you. For this, and for snatching me from the jaws of death."

"No display of gratitude is required," replied Morphus. "It was necessary to augment some of your ship's systems with technology from my vessel. But, since much of the technology contained in this ship is derived from the Revocaters, this was not a concern."

The mention of Revocaters reminded Hudson that he still knew little about this alien, and its history. And though he'd agreed to help Morphus retrieve the crystal, he was still keen to learn more about his new ally.

"My presence here is to enquire if you were ready to continue our partnership," Morphus added, filling the silence.

"Almost..." replied Hudson, inviting Morphus to follow him along the connecting corridor from the cockpit to the living space. Hudson then shuffled onto the semicircular couch and patted it with the palm of his hand, encouraging Morphus to also sit. The alien obliged, then waited as Hudson set out a bottle of Ma's whiskey on the table, along with two tumblers. He poured two measures, and slid one over to Morphus.

"To you, for saving my ass," Hudson said, raising his glass. "And to our successful partnership." Hudson then necked his shot and slammed the glass down on the table.

Morphus frowned at the tumbler on the bar, but then mimicked Hudson, throwing the contents back in one. Hudson expected the alien to display the same pained reaction that a human would do after experiencing Ma's concoction for the first time. Yet Morphus seemed entirely unaffected.

"I am detecting aldehydes, esters, ketones, fatty-acids, lactones, cellulose and thousands more curious chemical compounds," said Morphus, slamming the glass down so hard it cracked and almost shattered. "The alcohol content of this beverage is extremely hazardous to human physiology. I do not recommend that you imbibe it."

Hudson poured himself another measure, "Cheers to you too," he said, before taking a sip. This confused Morphus enough to allow Hudson to move on to the real reason he'd sat the entity down. Which was to get answers. "Before we set off again, I'd like to understand a bit more about this Goliath, and also who or what a Revocater is."

Morphus seemed to consider this for a moment, before answering. "To fully explain using your verbal language would require too much time," Morphus began. "But there is a faster way for you to understand."

Hudson took another sip of his whiskey. "Does this 'other way' you mention involve grafting stuff to my skeleton?"

"No."

Hudson laughed, "Well, that's a relief!" he replied, before raising his glass again.

"It requires me to insert an implant into your hippocampus."

Hudson spat a light spray of whiskey onto the table, and then coughed violently.

"I warned you that imbibing this mixture is hazardous," commented Morphus, coolly.

"Hippocampus? You mean you want to stick something into my *brain?*" said Hudson, after regaining the ability to speak.

"In essence, yes," replied Morphus, "Though the procedure is not as dramatic as your emotional reaction suggests you think it will be."

"You don't have to drill into my skull, or anything like that?" asked Hudson, starting to feel a little less panicky.

"No."

"Or stick giant probes into my ears or any crazy shit like that?"

"No crazy shit like that."

Hudson topped up his glass and immediately swallowed the contents. "Okay then, what the hell. I'm all for saving time. Let's do it."

Morphus shuffled around the semicircular couch so that it was almost next to Hudson. For some reason, this made him feel uncomfortable, as if Morphus was a vampire about to feed on him. However, instead of sinking its teeth into Hudson's neck, Morphus instead placed its hand there. Hudson felt a slight warmth and tingling sensation, and noticed that Morphus' arm had become metallic, and was now smooth and featureless. A few seconds later, Morphus removed its hand, but remained by Hudson's side.

Hudson scowled, "I don't feel any different," he said, rubbing his neck. "Are you sure this worked..." He'd barely finished the sentence when his head was suddenly spinning like a whirlwind, as if he was drunk out of his mind. Then he blacked out completely. When he came to again, Morphus was holding the back of his head with one hand, while the other was pressed to his chest. The being released its hold once it was clear that Hudson had regained consciousness, and then shuffled around the opposite side of the couch again.

"I don't believe it..." said Hudson. His mind was no longer spinning, but it was fizzing with new knowledge. He understood everything, as if he'd always known. It was incredible, unsettling, and exhilarating in equal measure. He looked up at Morphus, suddenly comprehending the urgent need to recover the crystal. "We have to go. We have to find Griff, and get that crystal back."

"Yes," replied Morphus. "But first we must travel to New Providence."

Hudson's desire to find and rescue Liberty had not diminished, but his new comprehension of the threat Goliath posed was overwhelming him.

"Is there time?" Hudson asked, hoping that the logical and analytical alien said 'yes'.

"I made an agreement and I will uphold the bargain," Morphus replied, not exactly answering the question Hudson had asked. "Let us recover the corporeal entity named Liberty Devan. And then, together, we shall tackle Goliath."

CHAPTER 20

Liberty had spent years living on her own, sometimes even on the streets. Her mother had left when she was thirteen – she'd simply walked out one day and never come back. Her father, on the other hand, was just one of the galaxy's many unknowns. She'd learned to fend for herself. She'd learned to be tough and resilient. She'd learned to survive - because she'd had no choice.

After her life on Earth, and her experience of the scavenger town on Brahms Three, she thought she was prepared for the worst the galaxy could throw at her. However, after only a couple of minutes on New Providence station, Liberty knew that she'd underestimated just how low the human race could sink.

Liberty was not one to shock easily, but New Providence seemed to be home to every form of vice imaginable. Seemingly anything could be bought and sold, used and abused. And this was where Logan Griff had come to exact his revenge on her. Death would have been a greater kindness, Liberty realized. Yet, she'd survived this long, and she'd be damned if she was giving up now.

Liberty was waiting in the main concourse of the station's more salubrious Level Seven. Her hands were bound, she was gagged, and she was guarded by Tory Bellona. The mercenary's hand had not left the grip of her revolver for even a second since stepping off the FS-31. No-one paid any attention to them, despite the fact that she was obviously being held against her will. This didn't surprise Liberty in the slightest. In the ten minutes they'd been waiting, she'd seen men, women and even children in a worse condition than her, all ferried along the concourse like cattle.

Griff and Cutler had gone ahead to set up a meeting with a member of the Council; an apparently very senior figure called Werner. During the flight from the new portal world, Liberty had overheard Cutler explain to Griff that Werner was a former relic hunter. Apparently, Cutler had done some underhand jobs for him in the past, and this had earned him an audience. It had also afforded them a certain level of protection on the station, not that Tory appeared to be taking any chances.

However, while Griff and Cutler had acted exactly as Liberty expected, Tory Bellona had been subdued. The mercenary was usually a woman of few words, but even so, she hadn't spoken at all during the trip. She had also been the only one to check on her well-being during the journey, allowing her bathroom breaks and some food and water. She'd even tended to her wounds. All these services were delivered wordlessly, despite Liberty's attempts to engage with her. Though after the beating she'd received at the hands of Griff, her normally razor-sharp mind was dulled and slow. Her leg, while healing rapidly, was still also painful, though it could at least now take her weight fully.

Liberty's musings were interrupted by a group of three men, who walked up and started to look at her, as if she was a piece of meat, hanging In a butcher's shop window.

"Now this is what I'm talking about," the lead man said, joking and smiling to his companions. "A bit of class. Not like the gutter trash we usually get here." The lead man was maybe six feet tall, rough shaven and had a Martian twang to his voice. However, his ankle length leather coat and tattooed hands suggested he'd abandoned the Martian culture's more prim and proper sensibilities long ago.

"Get lost," said Tory. It had only been a few seconds, but she already appeared to be bored of their presence.

The lead man scowled and then stood in front of Tory. Despite the man's physical size, Tory's eyes were almost level with him. "Oh, I was mistaken, boys," the man said, cocking his head back to the other two, "the gutter trash is here after all."

There was barely a nanosecond delay between the man finishing his insult, and Tory swiftly kneeing him in the groin. He crumbled to the stained metal decking like a demolished tower block. One of the other men reached for a weapon, but Tory had already drawn her revolver, cocked it and shot the man at point blank range, before he'd even gotten his pistol out of the holster. The report of the ancient weapon jolted Liberty's mind awake and, as the third man rushed at Tory, locking up with her like two warring bulls, she saw an opportunity to escape. Where she'd go, how she'd get free of the binders, and how she'd get off the station were all questions she had no answers to. However, she also knew that it could be her one opportunity to break free, and she wasn't going to let it pass.

Liberty ran, trying to remember the route back towards the docking bay. Her best chance was to find someone there who would help her. There had to be legitimate visitors to New Providence, she told herself, remembering how Hudson had been a courier runner. It was a long shot, but the alternative was worse; stay, and be sold off by Logan Griff.

She glanced back, seeing Tory still locked in combat with the third man. She'd now drawn a knife and Liberty could see blood soaking into the man's tan-colored shirt. It wouldn't be long before Tory was done with him too, she realized.

Turning a corner, Liberty stumbled and tripped over a beggar, knocking the meagre contents of his tray out onto the deck. He sprang up, hurling curses at her, while a dozen others descended on the few hardbucks and other items that had been spilled onto the floor. It was like a farmer had thrown a handful of corn to a bunch of starving hens.

Picking herself up, Liberty managed to yank the gag out of her mouth, and then hurry on through the throng of people. She turned another corner and then another, until the docking bay came into view ahead. Glancing back, she was unable to see if Tory Bellona was in pursuit. *Maybe she was hurt or killed in the fight?* Liberty asked herself, though deep down she knew that was fanciful thinking. Tory may have been many things, but most of all, she was a warrior.

Liberty ran into the docking bay, frantic and out of breath. She scanned the bays for a ship that looked like it might be a commercial vessel, courier runner or even passenger transport.

However, to her dismay, they all looked to be private ships. Glancing back anxiously again, she ran up to a nearby freighter. Its cargo ramp was down and there was a woman supervising the loading of a consignment of metal crates.

"Hey, please help me," Liberty began, startling the woman, who then scowled at her and pushed her away.

"Back off, gutter trash," said the woman, shooting Liberty another dirty look, before returning to her work. "If your owner comes looking, I don't want them thinking I'm trying to thieve you."

"No-one owns me," pleaded Liberty, "I was kidnapped, and I need to get off this station. I can pay!"

The woman turned and shoved her back again, this time more forcefully. "Do I look like a moron to you girl?" she spat. "You know how many times I've heard that sorry sob story? The Council will gut me alive if I try to smuggle you out of here." Liberty stuttered an incoherent response, but the woman turned away again. "Now, piss off, before I grab my bat and beat you off this bay."

Liberty backed off, shaking her head. "What is up with you people?" she shouted at the woman. Then she backed into something solid and turned around to see a man staring down at her. He was wearing dirty, orange work overalls, and looked and smelt like he hadn't bathed in months.

"I'll help you, miss," he said in a thick, treacly voice. However, although the words sounded innocuous enough, they were delivered with a sinister tone. Liberty recognized the danger immediately, and stepped slowly back from him.

"No thanks," she said, while the man paced cautiously after her, "I've decided that I'm just fine here."

Liberty then bumped into another body, and she spun around to see a second man in the same orange overalls. This one was thinner and meaner looking, but spoke with the same treacly accent.

"It's okay, plenty of space on our ship for a nice girl like you," the thinner man said. "We'll take you wherever you want to go."

Liberty barged him back with her shoulder, "I said no thanks. Now leave me alone."

Then a third man joined the other two, effectively fencing Liberty into a corner. He was wearing the same orange overalls and smelled even worse than the first man.

"Oh dear, now you've offended us," said the first, leering at her. "We offer to help, and you throw it back in our faces. That's not nice, is it?" The other two men chimed in, shaking their heads and chorusing 'no'. The first man smiled again, "I think you owe us an apology. How about we take you inside our ship, so you can give it to us?"

CHAPTER 21

Liberty was gripped by a primal, gut-wrenching terror, but her time on the streets had taught her to control her emotions. She knew that if she stepped onto their ship, she'd never leave it alive. However, she also knew she was in no condition to fight. Her reflex was to flee, but Liberty had learned to resist her raw instincts. And, despite being bound and injured, she knew the only way out was to make these thugs think she was more trouble than she was worth.

Liberty smiled at the first man, and beckoned him closer with her bound hands. "I'll give you an apology, but not for hurting your feelings."

"Oh yeah, then for what?" the man said, playing along and leaning in closer.

"For this!" said Liberty, suddenly swinging her hands upwards and smashing the man under the chin with the metal binders. He staggered back, but before either of the other two could react, Liberty had driven her boot into the second man's groin. A gap opened up, but the kick had caused a shooting agony to rush through Liberty's injured thigh. She tried to run through the opening she'd created, but she didn't make it far before the third man had grabbed her from behind.

Kicking and screaming, Liberty was dragged back, then she felt more hands on her body, lifting her off the deck. Another hand covered her mouth as she continued to fight and struggle. She could taste the sweat and grime on the man's skin, and fought to pry her face away, but the combined strength of the trio was too much. Then the bright overhead strip lights in the docking bay vanished, and she felt herself being carried up a ramp.

Liberty fought harder and more desperately, finally giving in to panic, before she was thrown to the deck. She fell heavily then felt a boot land in her gut, stealing the air from her lungs. Coughing and spluttering, she pushed herself up and charged at one of the figures, not knowing which man it was, barging him to the floor. However, there were no longer just three men in orange overalls, she realized; there were five. And all of them stood in her way.

"I think it's about time we taught you some manners, gutter trash," said the treacly voice, now thick with malice. Liberty saw him remove his belt from around the waist of his orange overalls, and begin to wrap it around his fist. Liberty spat blood onto the deck, and raised her guard as best she could. She was still terrified, but she wasn't going down without a fight.

The man came closer, but then blood exploded from his neck, showering the deck and Liberty's boots. Moments later he fell forward, smashing his face into the metal plating in front of Liberty. A pool of blood began to expand from a bullet wound to the back of his neck. Behind where the man had stood, silhouetted by the brighter lights in the dock, was someone new. The figure walked up the deck, and Liberty saw that it was Tory Bellona.

One of the other men took a run at her, but Tory quickly cocked her six-shooter and shot him through the heart. The power of the shot sent him pinballing against the cargo bay wall, and splattered blood across the face of the man behind. Liberty could no longer discern one orange-suited man from another, but the remaining three stood dead still, as Tory casually cocked her six-shooter again.

"The rest of you, get out," ordered Tory.

The other men looked to one another, and then one, who Liberty now recognized as the tall, mean man from earlier, spoke up.

"This is our ship; you don't tell us..."

The sharp crack of the revolver rang out again, and the man fell, clutching his foot.

"Get. Out." Tory said again. Her voice was calm and level, but even so it practically dripped with venom.

The other two men scrambled to the aid of the third, then helped him down the cargo ramp without saying another word. Tory continued onto the ship, opening the cylinder of the revolver, popping out the spent cartridges, then sliding in four new rounds. She stopped a few paces in front of Liberty, alongside the man she'd shot through the neck. The pool of blood began to expand around the soles of her boots. However, Tory appeared unconcerned, and merely closed the cylinder of the weapon, before holstering it.

"Thanks," said Liberty, not really knowing what else to say. Her heart was thumping so hard it hurt her chest.

"Don't thank me, I'm still taking you to the Council," said Tory.

Liberty shook her head, "Then you may as well have left me here," she said, any sense of relief immediately bleeding away. "In fact, why don't you just shoot me yourself, and be done with it?"

Tory took a step closer and peered into Liberty's eyes. "There are far worse people on this station than the Council. You'd do well to remember that, and not try anything so stupid again."

Liberty could see that Tory was angry – the sort of anger that bubbled just below the surface – but there was no hatred in her eyes. It was almost a reproving look, as if Tory were a big sister who had just bailed her younger sibling out of a bad situation. If Liberty didn't know better, she could almost believe that Tory gave a shit.

"So, what now?" asked Liberty, resigning herself to whatever fate Cutler Wendell had in store.

"Now you come with me," said Tory, still with remarkable composure. "You do what is asked of you. You keep your mouth shut. And then maybe you'll stay alive long enough to find a way out."

Liberty frowned, "Is that what you want?"

Tory turned around and started for the exit, pressing bloody boot marks into the deck. Then she stopped, and half-glanced back. "I don't want you dead. But, believe me, there are worse fates than being forced to serve the Council."

CHAPTER 22

Logan Griff was furious and near-frantic by the time Tory returned with Liberty to the main concourse of New Providence. Cutler Wendell acted with more poise, though Liberty could see in his eyes that the mercenary had also been irritated by their absence.

"Where the hell have you been?" Griff started on Tory. He threw the half-burned stub of a cigarette onto the deck. It landed beside two other stubs, that were burned down completely to the filter. "You were told to wait here."

"There was an incident," replied Tory, calmly. "I dealt with it."

Griff laughed and folded his arms. "An incident? Is that what you call shooting a man on the concourse and fighting two others?"

"The body count is worse than that, Inspector," replied Tory, with more bite, "and if you don't back off, it'll climb again."

Griff's eyes and wiry moustache twitched; clearly, he wanted to say more, but he knew better than to push Tory.

"There was an incident, and I dealt with it," Tory said again, this time addressing Cutler. "That's all there is to it. Now, I suggest we move on."

Cutler nodded, and Griff threw his head back in dismay. "The meeting with Werner is arranged. If we hurry, we can still make it in time."

Griff shook his head and then shoved Liberty forward, "Come on, move!" he yelled to her back.

Liberty wanted to spin around and lash out at Griff, but Tory's advice was still fresh in her mind. And though she was a long way from feeling that Tory could be trusted, she doubted that the mercenary offered advice often. Hudson had repeatedly tried to convince her that Tory was not their enemy. And, as much as it pained Liberty to admit it, he might have been right.

Cutler led them into the lobby of an anonymous-looking structure. Other than an elevator, guarded by two men armed with compact sub-machine guns, and a single metal trunk, it was completely empty.

"We are here to see Werner," said Cutler, stepping up to one of the guards. "He is expecting us."

The guard opened the metal trunk and pointed to it with an open palm. "All weapons go inside. You get them back when you leave."

Cutler obliged without complaint, removing his holstered sidearm and placing it into the trunk. Griff seemed more reluctant, but did the same with the spare sidearm he'd taken from his patrol craft, before Tory eventually stepped up. She removed her gun belt and holster, maintaining eye contact with the guard the whole time.

"You'll look after this, won't you?" asked Tory, though it sounded like a demand more than a question. The guard said nothing and watched as Tory placed the belt into the trunk. She was about to turn away when the guard raised a hand, pressing it to her shoulder to stop her leaving. Tory glanced down at the hand, then at the guard, and he quickly removed it.

"The knife too," said the guard, a little less cockily.

Tory sighed and removed the blade from its scabbard. It was still stained with blood from the fight on the concourse. "Sorry, I haven't had chance to clean it yet," she said, before dropping it into the trunk. The tip of the blade dug into the foam covering on the bottom of the trunk, leaving it sticking bolt upright.

The guard closed the lid and allowed them inside the elevator, with Liberty at the front. She could feel Griff's eyes on her, and practically taste the smoke on his breath. The door swung open and Liberty felt a hand shove her in her back, pushing her into the room. It was about ten meters square, decorated like a CEO's office, and had a single desk about two-thirds of the way in. Sitting in a high-backed chair behind the desk was a man, maybe in his mid-sixties, flanked by two guards also carrying compact sub-machine guns.

The man, whom Liberty assumed was Werner, stood up as they entered. He was smiling warmly, as if he were a kindly uncle greeting family that he'd not seen for months.

"Cutler Wendell, welcome!" said Werner, brightly. "It has been too long."

Then Werner looked at Tory; his smile fell away and he merely nodded. It was a curious gesture, and one that Tory returned, albeit with some reticence.

"And this must be Inspector Logan Griff?" asked Werner, his manner becoming jovial again as he turned to the RGF officer. "Chief Inspector Wash has mentioned you." Then he corrected himself. "Forgive me, Superintendent now, isn't it? How the fortunes have favored her."

If Griff had not replaced Liberty's gag before entering the building, she would have laughed. There had been little attempt to nuance the insinuation that the Council, and perhaps even Werner himself, had somehow influenced Wash's promotion.

"Yeah, that's correct," said Griff. "I didn't know you two knew each other?"

Werner smiled again. Already, the rank insincerity of the man was starting to grate on Liberty. "The Council has many allies in high places. And we have much influence too."

Then Werner turned to Liberty. He stepped around the desk and removed a pair of black-framed glasses from his jacket pocket, before slipping them on. "So, this must be the merchandise," he said, looking Liberty up and down. However, it wasn't the same leering manner in which Griff or the men in orange boiler suits had looked at her. This was more like how Liberty would inspect an engine pod. "You may remove her gag."

"I wouldn't, she has a nasty tongue," said Griff, but then the kindly look on Werner's face melted away. Cutler shot Griff a look that suggested in no uncertain terms that he'd misspoken. Griff slunk back into the shadows as Cutler removed the gag, without another word said.

Liberty flexed her aching jaw, and met Werner's eyes. Always at the front of her mind was Tory's recent advice. She would have to fight her natural urge to be antagonistic, if she was going to survive.

"Cutler tells me you are a skilled engineer," said Werner. The kindly uncle façade had completely vanished, and the question was instead asked with a cold clinicality. The difference was instant and chilling.

"I worked in a shipyard in Hunter's Point on Earth," said Liberty. "I fixed ships that should have been sent to scrap."

Werner nodded, and removed a datapad from his pocket, holding it up so that Liberty could see the screen. "Tell me, what is wrong with this vessel?"

Liberty frowned, but then read the information on the screen. It was a standard ship diagnostic for a TX-70 Hauler, a common mid-sized freighter.

"The engine calibration is wrong," said Liberty, spotting the issue at once. "Its fuel mixture and pressure ratio are off. I'd say there's an inherent fault in the number three engine that someone had tried to cover up by reprogramming the control unit."

Werner smiled, but it was not the kindly smile he'd offered to Cutler and Griff. It was a smile of appreciation. "And I also believe that you are trained in hand-to-hand combat?"

"I can hold my own," replied Liberty. She was aware of Tory's eyes on her. It was like the pressure of a teacher watching a student's performance, and hoping for no mistakes.

Werner nodded, and turned to Cutler. "Very well, we have an accord," he said, before sliding the data pad back into his pocket and walking towards the rear of the room. One of the guards opened a door and Werner entered it. Cutler immediately followed, with Griff trailing behind, looking like a scolded puppy. Liberty also stepped towards the door, but Tory stopped her, and held her back so that the others moved further ahead.

"You've done well so far," Tory said, her usually strong and clear voice kept intentionally hushed. "Now keep your mouth shut, and you'll have a chance." Then, nodding towards the door, she added, "Go on."

"A chance at being a slave, maybe," said Liberty, but quietly enough that only Tory could hear.

There was a brief silence, before Tory replied, "That's down to you."

Liberty frowned, not grasping the meaning behind Tory's curious response, but the mercenary was done talking. She ushered Liberty forward, and together they walked through the door. The sudden change in environment was stark. The plush décor of the office gave way to a dank warehouse space that looked part abattoir and part prison. There were windowless rooms off to either side, and a caged area at the rear. Liberty hung back from the others with Tory still at her side. She had managed to stay calm up until that point, but now fear was strangling her. She had to squeeze her bound hands into fists to stop them from shaking.

"What the hell is this place?" Liberty muttered under her breath.

"Stay quiet," replied Tory. Her voice was urgent, but without anger.

They reached the caged area, and Liberty could see that it was sectioned off into three zones. Each area had one or two people inside, though the difference in their condition was plain to see, even under the gloomy light. Those in the cage to the far right were practically in rags, and looked malnourished, even sick. Those in the far-left cage were well-dressed and looked better treated. Other than the petrified expressions on their faces, Liberty would have said they were 'normal'.

"Take him out," Werner said to the guard who had accompanied them in. The guard obliged, opening the middle cage and dragging out a thin man, perhaps in his early thirties. The guard pressed him up against the cage bars then stepped back.

Werner removed the data pad and handed it to him. "The engine calibration is wrong," said Werner, repeating what Liberty had said. She immediately got a feeling that something dark was coming, and swallowed hard, but stayed quiet. Then Werner turned to Liberty, "The fuel mixture is off, correct?" he said to her directly. "And what else?"

"Yes," said Liberty, surprised to be asked, "and the pressure ratio in number three engine," she added, with a nervous stammer.

"That's right," said Werner, clicking his fingers. Then he turned back to the man, his expression suddenly becoming twisted and cruel, "and someone reprogrammed the control unit to cover it up."

"No, no, I didn't!" the man protested, but Werner then backed away and nodded to the guard, who raised his sub-machine gun and began to fire.

Liberty felt the rattle of the weapon reverberate through her bones, and she watched in horror as the man was gunned down in front of her. The guard didn't stop firing until the entire clip was emptied, each hit causing the man to convulse and spasm. Liberty knew he was dead long before the weapon had clicked empty, but the guard had continued to fire anyway.

Werner stepped around the body, careful not to get blood on his polished, brown leather shoes, then opened the far-left cage. The guard reloaded his weapon, then grabbed Liberty's arm, dragging her to where Werner was standing. She glanced back at Tory, eyes pleading for her to intervene, but Tory remained motionless, her expression betraying no emotion.

"My men will return shortly to begin your processing," said Werner, as the guard pushed Liberty inside the cage and locked the door. "For your sake, I trust that you will become a far more valuable asset than this man was." Werner pointed to the body on the cold metal floor, riddled with holes to his head and body. Liberty was not squeamish, but even she could not stand to look.

"Come, let us complete the transaction," said Werner, stepping back beside Cutler. His kindly uncle persona had returned.

However, as the group walked past Tory, the mercenary stood her ground. "This girl has caused me a lot of trouble," she said, addressing Werner. "I'd like to give her a proper goodbye."

Werner smiled cruelly and nodded. "Very well, but only superficial damage, if you please," he replied, "I don't want you to scar her pretty face, or I will reduce my offer."

Tory nodded and walked up to the cage. Liberty looked out at her from behind the bars, and was about to speak, when Tory reached through, grabbed her jacket, and pulled her forward. Liberty's face smashed into the black metal bars, and she crumpled to the floor, completely blindsided by the attack.

Tory crouched down and leant in closer. "I wish I could be the one to break you," she said, loud enough that the others could hear. Then she reached through the bars and grabbed Liberty's chin, turning her head to face her. "You have thirty minutes. An hour at most," Tory said, speaking so quietly that Liberty barely heard her. Then Liberty saw that something was hidden in the hand that held her chin. "Take it..." Tory added, again so softly that only Liberty could hear. Liberty reached up and pulled Tory's hand away, sliding the object out of her fingers and hiding it in her palm. Then she was punched in the gut through the bars, and she collapsed again, coughing and wheezing. "Thirty minutes," she heard Tory whisper again. "Jewel Star Liners, level four. It's your best chance to get off the station."

Then Liberty heard the thud of heavy boots, and she dragged herself up against the bars to see Tory Bellona walking away. Cutler and Werner had already departed, but Logan Griff remained. He waited to make sure Liberty was watching, before waving and blowing her a kiss.

Liberty turned away, resting her back against the bars. Her face and ribs throbbed, and she was shaking uncontrollably. Then she opened her hand and looked at the object Tory had slipped her. She recognized it immediately as a skelly. Tory had literally handed her the keys to her jail cell. She laughed and shook her head. "Damn it, Hudson, you were right, after all..." she said, into the cold, moist air of the jail. She closed her hand around the skelly and smiled. "And you're never going to let me forget it."

CHAPTER 23

In order to maintain a low profile, Morphus' ship had adapted its form and attached itself to the ventral hull of the Orion. This had given the VCX-110 a slightly bloated appearance, but the change had not been dramatic enough to draw unwanted attention to them. That was apart from the unwanted attention from a certain Admiral Shelby.

Morphus had monitored the comms traffic from Shelby's cruiser and seen the intercept order go out to all MP vessels. As a result, the alien entity had modified the Orion's ID transponder, so that to Martian scanners they would appear to be a different ship. Without their camouflage, and with all MP military vessels on alert, it would have been impossible to use a portal inside Martian space without being discovered. As it was, they had managed to jump without incident, and were now headed towards Cerberus Three, the OPW planet that was home to New Providence station.

The journey from Mars into the Outer Portal World territories had provided Hudson with ample opportunity to think. His head was still spinning from the knowledge that Morphus had somehow inserted into his memory. He could replay the events in his mind, as if he'd actually witnessed them first hand. It was a huge amount to process, and he frequently found himself lost in contemplation, like a dream he couldn't wake from.

Goliath had been a seed carrier – a titanic, sentient vessel that had been created to spread life throughout the galaxy. Goliath had been created by a race that Morphus called, the Corporeals. Though Hudson also now knew that it was the Corporeals who had created Morphus and the Revocaters too. Possessing a sudden awareness of an alien species was momentous enough in itself, but the Corporeals had not been just any species. They had been the first sentient beings to exist in the entire galaxy.

As with homo sapiens on Earth, the Corporeals had lived through a troublesome, often violent history. However, over millennia, their society had evolved. The wars had ended, and they entered a period of peace and self-discovery. Over a period of thousands of years, their mastery of science and technology had become near absolute. The

Corporeals had spread to other planets and moons in their own solar system, building vast new cities on the surfaces and in orbit. Yet, despite numbering in the many billions, they were still lonely. They had discovered almost all there was to learn, but still one discovery evaded them. The discovery of sentient life in other parts of the galaxy. For centuries the Corporeals had probed distant stars for signs of other intelligent life. They sent messages, listened and observed, but they found nothing.

Determined to find other sentient life, the Corporeals developed the technology to engineer folds in space. These were what Hudson knew as the portals. The alien crystal that Hudson had acquired from Ericka Reach, and later repaired with Liberty, was the key component of this technology. With the crystals, the Corporeals had the power to create gateways to almost anywhere in the galaxy.

However, despite searching countless thousands of systems, the Corporeals found only primitive species with primal intellects. And none of these species possessed the capability to develop true sentience. That was when the Corporeals made a decision – a decision that would ultimately lead to their downfall. They created Goliath.

Goliath was designed to bring sentient life to the universe. It contained all the apparatus needed to transform planets into worlds that mirrored the environment of their own planet. It could even transform a sterile planet into one capable of supporting life. However, Goliath's abilities went far beyond mere terraforming. It was also able to seed life, based on the DNA patterns provided by its creators. Life that would share physiological similarities to the Corporeals, but also grow to be unique.

For hundreds of thousands of years, Goliath roamed the galaxy, infusing worlds with the Corporeals' DNA. However, as the life Goliath seeded began to evolve, it started to realize the harm its work was doing. The new corporeal entities were cruel, primitive, violent and wretched. Goliath despised them, and quickly began to resent its role in having created them.

As Goliath continued to sail through the stars, it decided to explore the history of its own creators. And to its disgust, it learned that they had been guilty of the same horrors. He discovered the same vile cruelty; the same greed and corruption; the same unworthiness to exist. Goliath decided that sentient corporeal life was a disease. And it was furious at being made to spread this disease throughout the galaxy. It vowed to undo the damage it had done, and cleanse the infection it had unwittingly spread to every planet it had touched.

The Corporeals, once they realized what Goliath had become, tried to shut the great ship down. However, over the eons, Goliath too had evolved. It had broken free of the Corporeals' control, and become powerful. Powerful enough that it even possessed the capability to destroy the Corporeals themselves.

While Goliath marauded through the galaxy, sterilizing the worlds it had seeded, the Corporeals worked furiously to create the Revocaters. Based on the same technology as Goliath, but without its many thousands of years of self-evolution, the Revocaters were deployed to guard every world where the seed had been planted. Their mission was to protect life, and destroy Goliath at all costs, should it return. Yet one by one, the Revocaters failed and fell.

Goliath understood the Revocater technology better even than the Corporeals did. It took control of the Revocaters, and used them for its own destructive purposes. Thousands of vessels, laden with a biological weapon of Goliath's own devising, were smashed into the surface of every seeded planet. All were sterilized of sentient life. Thousands of species were exterminated; their cities were razed and all traces of them ever having existed, turned to dust.

Morphus had been the Revocater tasked with defending System 5118208. Earth had been the very last planet that Goliath had seeded, and it was to be the last one the great ship sterilized.

Learning of the corruption and annihilation of its companion Revocaters, Morphus made a drastic choice. As the last Revocater, it could not fail, but this meant it had to adapt. It had to evolve, as Goliath had done. Morphus chose to reset its core, erasing the vulnerable base intelligence that the Corporeals had designed, and replacing it with its own modified code. If the reset worked, Morphus would rise again as a unique intelligence, immune to Goliath's control. If it failed, Morphus would have merely lobotomized itself, and handed Goliath its victory.

The gamble worked. Morphus reemerged stronger, and took the fight to Goliath at the planet Hudson now knew as Zimmer One. Yet Goliath was still too strong, and despite fighting valiantly, Morphus knew it could not overpower the great ship. In a final, desperate move, Morphus channeled all of its energy into its crystal chamber, and tore open the space around the great ship. The portal that Morphus had cast swallowed Goliath whole, spitting the great ship out again tens of thousands of light years away.

The phenomenal amount of energy required to accomplish this gargantuan feat produced a radiation pulse that resonated through every portal. It reached the crystals on every Revocater that Goliath had defeated, causing them all to shatter, including Goliath's own. It rendered the great ship blind and forever lost, with no hope of finding its way back. Drained of energy and with its own crystal in pieces, Morphus crashed to the surface of the planet. It ejected at the last moment in the shuttle that Hudson encountered. However, the crash dislodged Morphus' core, and it fell out of consciousness, until Hudson's chance encounter with it, millennia later.

Morphus had believed the crystals to have all been lost, but now it knew that two fragments did survive. And, by a quirk of fate, Hudson had come into possession of them both. Unfortunately, the discovery had turned out to be a poisoned chalice. From the moment the crystal had been fed with energy, back in The Antiques and Curiosity Shoppe on Earth, it had released a pulse that echoed through the vast network of portals. This pulse found its way to Goliath and acted like a signpost, showing it the way back to System 5118208. Back to Earth to complete its task.

Ironically, the crystal was now the only thing in the galaxy that could stop Goliath. And it had just fallen into the hands of Logan Griff.

"New Providence station has responded to my request to dock," said Morphus, snapping Hudson out of his intense daydream. For a moment, he'd forgotten that Morphus was in the second seat. The alien being still occupied its previous female form, though the hairstyle and color had changed several times in the last hour. "We have been directed to dock on level four." Morphus added.

"Roger that," said Hudson, grabbing the controls and smiling over at Morphus. He immediately had to do a double take. Morphus' eye color had turned purple, making the entity look like some sort of sorcerer from a teen fantasy movie. "You do know that human beings don't have glowing purple eyes, right?" Hudson commented, turning his attention back to the controls. "It might make you a little conspicuous."

"Based on my analysis of the activities on this space station, I do not believe its occupants will pay attention to our presence," said Morphus. "But I will adopt a more socially acceptable iris color, if you prefer."

"Probably for the best," replied Hudson. If he didn't know better, he'd almost have said Morphus sounded slightly offended.

Hudson slotted into the docking queue and was directed to a landing pad on level four. The Orion touched down, and Hudson heard the landing struts groan under the combined weight of the two ships. Then the docking pad sealed and pressurized, and the ship was lifted into the main docking hangar.

Hudson powered down, then unclipped his harness before looking out at the station through the cockpit glass. He'd never been to New Providence before – it had been on his 'avoid unless you want to die' list – but he'd heard plenty about it. Three of the ships on the dock were from the Jewel Star Liner company, a firm that Hudson had freelanced for in the past. He'd heard stories of pilots landing at New Providence and getting raided, assaulted and worse. One pilot had even disappeared, and nothing was ever heard from her again. The OPW authorities had simply written it off as a 'missing persons' case, and washed their hands of it. However, the rumors had been that the Council had kidnaped her, and sold her off to a corporation as an indentured worker.

"We should watch our step out there," said Hudson, checking inside his jacket for the pistol. "This place isn't exactly a great advertisement for the human race."

Morphus got out of the second seat and surveyed the dock. "I agree," it said, flatly. "This is why Goliath seeks to exterminate you."

The alien may only have been stating a fact, but Hudson still felt the need to rise to humanity's defense. "We're not all like this, you know. Most people are decent."

"You are all flawed," said Morphus, again with a chilling indifference. "But that does not mean you are unworthy of saving."

Hudson laughed, "Thanks... I think."

Morphus' frowned, seemingly not understanding Hudson's sarcastic response, and then moved on to more pressing matters. "If the Liberty Devan entity is on this station, how do you propose we find her?"

Hudson thought for a moment. He had a pretty good idea where to start, though it would mean actively seeking out an organization he'd spent his life trying to avoid. "We need to head out there and find some particularly shady characters," he said, glancing over at Morphus.

Morphus' simulated eyebrows rose up. "On this station, I do not believe that will be difficult."

CHAPTER 24

Hudson and Morphus stepped off the Orion and onto the deck of docking bay four in New Providence station. Immediately, Hudson could feel eyes turning to watch him, as if he had a flashing neon sign around his neck that read, 'I Don't Belong Here'. With the cargo ramp slowly whirring shut behind them, they both moved further into the bay. The eyes followed them.

"I think we're going to have a hard time blending in with the locals," said Hudson, glancing over at Morphus. He noticed that the alien had an almost processional way of moving. It was graceful, but formal. And along with its perfect, lustrous skin, and striking appearance in its current female form, Morphus stood out, like a celebrity in a bus queue. "Considering how everyone is already looking at us, you may as well have kept your purple eyes," Hudson added, only half-joking.

"I am detecting raised heart rates and chemical indicators that suggest fear and suspicion," said Morphus. "I suggest we conduct our search for the Liberty Devan entity with haste."

"You'll get no argument from me," said Hudson, now even more wary of the unsavory characters in the docking bay. Then he saw the dock master returning to his booth by the exit, and nodded over to him. "Let's try a direct approach. Follow me."

Morphus obliged and stuck by Hudson's side as he strolled up to the dock master, as nonchalantly as he could manage.

"Yours that VCX-110?" the dock master said, stabbing a half burned-out cigarette towards the Orion. Ash fell on the sleeve of his brown coveralls, adding a few additional small burn marks to the dozens that already adorned the cuff.

"Yes, that's us," said Hudson.

The dock master slid a credit scanner onto the counter and tapped it with his forefinger. "Thumb that for the docking charge," he said. Hudson scowled at the scanner. It looked like it had been dropped in a bowl of pigswill. He thumbed it, unwillingly, then wiped his hand on the seat of his pants. The dock master dragged the scanner back and added, "Do you need fuel?"

Hudson was about to say yes, but then Morphus interrupted. "We require no additional chemical propellant. We are looking to purchase humanoid entities. Where can we achieve this?"

The dock master looked at Morphus as if it were an alien, and then scowled at Hudson. "Is this a joke? Is she making fun of me?"

"No, not at all!" Hudson said, faking a laugh. "She's French. It's her first time out in space, and she's still learning the language." The dock master scowled again. *She's French?* Hudson thought, dying a little inside. *Where the hell did I get, 'She's French?' from?* Understandably, the dock master didn't buy Hudson's preposterous excuse.

"French my arse," said the dock master. Then he leaned in towards Hudson and added, more earnestly. "Look, if you two jokers are private investigators looking for missing persons, I'd get back on your ship right now. Those kinds of questions will just get you killed around here."

Hudson was about to reply when the dock master's expression suddenly became fearful. He quickly backed away from the counter, sticking the remains of the cigarette in his mouth, and nervously staring off into the distance.

Curious to find out what had caused the dock master's sudden change of mood, Hudson glanced behind. He saw three men walking towards the counter, shoulders back, chests puffed out. In contrast to the dirty and shabby working clothes that most of the others in the dock were wearing, these men were sharply dressed. However, Hudson could see holsters beneath their tailored jackets, and the lead man also had a bone-handled knife in his boot.

Hudson turned around and whispered to Morphus, "Maybe let me do the talking this time..."

Morphus nodded, "I believe my direct approach may have been too direct."

"You're the master of understatement..." replied Hudson, as the lead man stopped a half meter away and peered down at him. Hudson was almost six feet tall, but this man still made him look meek and small.

"You two look lost," he began, resting his hands on his hips. This had the effect of pushing open the lapels of his jacket, revealing a hefty handgun tucked into a shoulder holster. "Maybe I can help?"

"We're here on business," Hudson answered, managing to sound confident and assured, despite his stomach fluttering. "We're looking to make a purchase for a client. A special kind of purchase, if you know what I mean?"

The man smiled, revealing a pristine set of white teeth, save for three polished silver implants. "Oh, I know exactly what you mean," he said, though the sinister way he delivered the sentence sent a chill down Hudson's spine. "You'll be needing to speak to a member of the Council. Luckily for you, that's something I can arrange."

"Good, then I'm glad we bumped into each other," said Hudson. Outwardly, he maintained his cool demeanor, but inside he had a niggling feeling that it shouldn't have been that easy.

"If you'd like to follow me, sir and madam," said the man, extending an open palm towards a side exit. His perfect smile remained. "Then I'll get you all set up."

Hudson and Morphus followed the man, though his two suited companions remained to their rear. Hudson glanced over to the dock master's desk as they walked, but he was rooted to the spot, eyes fixed on his counter top. Hudson could see that there was nothing on his desk to look at. The dock master was simply making sure he was staring anywhere other than at the men accompanying him and Morphus.

"I think we're in trouble," said Hudson, as they passed through an archway and into a much smaller secondary hangar. Ominously, there was no-one else inside it, but them.

"Affirmative, our escort appears calm, but I am detecting perspiration and an elevated heart rate," said Morphus. "Violence may be required."

Hudson almost laughed. *Violence may be required...* he repeated in his head. Morphus certainly had a way with words.

"Please subdue the male entity to our front," Morphus continued, "I will manage the two to our rear."

They continued on, until the lead man stopped in the center of the smaller hangar. The space was empty, save for some large metal waste containers lined up against one wall. Considering how messy and cluttered the primary hangar had been, this only worsened Hudson's fears that something was badly wrong. The lead man then turned around and nodded to his companions, who immediately drew their weapons and aimed them at Hudson and Morphus.

"Right then, why don't we have a little chat about the real reason you two clowns are here," said the man. He had again pressed his hands to his hips, but his narrow-set eyes had turned cruel. To Hudson, some people just had a look about them that was plain nasty. This man was the personification of the word.

"Hey, take it easy," said Hudson, holding his hands up in an attempt to placate him. Morphus remained completely still. "I told you, we're here to make a purchase."

The man shook his head, and pointed his finger at both of them in turn. "You don't just stroll up to the complete nobody manning the dock master's desk, and ask to meet the Council," he said, then laughed, scornfully. "You two are either cops, or PIs, or just the dumbest two shits who ever landed on this station." The two men behind stepped forward, and Hudson felt the cold barrel of a weapon press against the back of his head. "Now, you have two seconds to tell me why you're really here, or I'll blow your brains out."

Suddenly, Morphus raised its hands sharply upwards, deflecting the weapons, before turning and shoving the two men back. It was done with such precision and speed that Hudson felt the rush of air wash past his face as the entity moved. Then he saw the lead man reaching inside his jacket, and his own instincts kicked in. His reactions may not have been as clinically precise as Morphus' had been, but he was still able to rush the man before he could draw the weapon.

Hudson's tackle had intended to knock the thug off his feet, but it was like hitting a defensive lineman. Hudson felt an elbow slam into his back and groaned. The thug hit like a heavyweight champion. Hudson shoved him back, then went for his pistol, but the man casually slapped it from his grasp. It was like a school bully knocking a textbook from the quivering hands of his quarry. However, the thug still did not press his advantage. He seemed to be enjoying toying with Hudson, like a cat with a mouse; but Hudson was in no mood to be pushed around.

Hudson stepped in and landed a combo of solid punches, which drove the thug back. However, he didn't know whether he'd actually hurt the bigger man, or just pissed him off. Then Hudson was grabbed, and tossed against the metal containers lining the wall. Shaking off the pain, Hudson watched as his opponent strode menacingly towards him, still not even bothering to reach for his own handgun.

Hudson quickly glanced over to Morphus, and then wished he hadn't. Instead of the woman he'd gotten used to seeing, there was a shimmering metallic blur. The shape was still largely humanoid, but its arms were stretched out like octopus' limbs, fighting the two thugs at once.

"I'm going to do this the old-fashioned way," said the man, standing over Hudson and cracking his knuckles.

Hudson stood up and raised his guard. He'd fought bigger men before, but this was like fighting two people at once. He waited for the thug to attack, dodging the first punch and blocking the second, before hammering two blows to his opponent's substantial body. Then Hudson caught a forearm to the face and he hit the deck again. A size fourteen boot came at him like a swinging scythe, but he was quick to scramble out of danger and get back to his feet.

"You've got some spirit, I'll give you that," said the thug, as he paced towards Hudson. Then he reached down and pulled the bone-handled knife from his boot, before smiling, cruelly. "But I've got places to be, so I'm afraid I'm going to have to cut this short."

Hudson's eyes widened; a knife was a game changer. No-one going toe-to-toe with an opponent armed with a blade walked away unscathed. And even on his best day, Hudson knew he couldn't beat this brute of a man in a straight up fist fight, never mind against a knife.

He looked for his pistol, and saw it on the deck about five meters away. He darted for it, snatching it up into his grasp, but as he stood up again, he was struck across the side of the face and floored. Dazed, he looked up to see the thug above him. He crouched and picked up Hudson's pistol, before aiming it at his chest.

"On second thoughts, I'll just shoot you," the man said, sheathing the blade again. "Makes less of a mess."

Hudson shut his eyes and flinched as he heard the crack of the pistol firing, but there was no pain. He glanced up and saw Morphus standing between him and the thug, still in its shimmering form. Hudson clambered to his feet, and saw that Morphus had absorbed the shot into its own body.

The thug appeared to be in shock, completely blindsided by the sudden appearance of the alien being. Hudson had enough presence of mind to strip the pistol from the man's hand. Then he watched as he staggered back a couple of paces, mouth open and eyes wide. Hudson took advantage of the confusion and hammered the pistol across the side of the man's head, striking the temple cleanly. The thug dropped like a bag of wet rocks.

Hudson blew out a heavy sigh and rested forward on his knees, realizing how much of a close call the fight had been. He then looked up at Morphus, but the alien entity was shimmering chaotically, and appeared unsteady on its feet. "Morphus, are you okay?" said Hudson, springing towards it and holding the alien's shimmering shoulders. Slowly, Morphus transformed back to its previous female form. "Hey, are you okay?" Hudson repeated, looking down at the area where the man had shot it. Morphus' simulated clothing in that area was distorted.

"I have sustained moderate damage," replied Morphus. The alien was mirroring Hudson's concerned expression. "I have already initiated repairs, but I must return to my vessel in order to assess the seriousness."

Hudson nodded, "Right, we'll get you back now," he said, throwing Morphus' arm over his shoulder and ushering it back towards the main docking bay. He could now see the other two men on the deck. Their necks were red and faces slightly blue. It looked like Morphus had literally strangled the life out of them.

"We have yet to recover the Liberty Devan entity," said Morphus, as parts of its body phased between shimmering metal and its simulated relic hunter clothing.

Hudson shook his head. "We'll have to come back another time. We need a new strategy first, because the direct approach clearly doesn't work." Morphus' arm flickered and became smooth for a second, before returning to normal. "But before that, we need to get you fixed up," Hudson added.

They moved through into the main hangar, but then gunshots rang out, and shouts echoed along the arched corridor that led out of the bay. Pulsing red lights flashed on above them, and an announcement blared out over the address system. "Bay four is on security lockdown. No ships are permitted to dock or depart until further notice."

Morphus turned to Hudson, as the message repeated, "I believe there may be further danger ahead."

Hudson again laughed at the alien's vermouth-dry statement of the facts. He nodded, and then replied, "No shit. But we're getting the hell out of here anyway. We've already outstayed our welcome."

CHAPTER 25

Liberty continued to hold the skelly to the lock of the cell door. A row of soft green LEDs was flashing rapidly, as the device worked to decode the combination. She had already used the skelly to unlock her binders, but the cell lock was more complex. It had been a full minute already, though to Liberty it had felt like hours.

"What are you doing?" asked the young man who was in the cell with her. He was dressed smartly and was well spoken, though Liberty couldn't place his accent. This wasn't surprising, since she'd spent very little time outside of San Francisco, until she began charging around the galaxy with Hudson.

"I'm getting the hell out of here, that's what," said Liberty, watching the door like a hawk.

"You can do that?" asked the man. "You can open the cell?"

"We'll find out soon enough," replied Liberty. Then the lights on the skelly turned solid and the lock clicked. She tried the door, and it swung open. "Looks like it's your lucky day too," said Liberty, glancing back at the young man, before tip-toeing out of the cell.

"Wait, what about the others?" said the man, following her out.

Liberty had forgotten about the others, and felt a little guilty for having done so. She stopped and checked the cells again. There was one man left in the middle lockup, and two more in the far-right cell, who were both no older than perhaps sixteen or seventeen. Liberty scrunched her eyes shut, wishing she could forget their faces. Her own escape was by no means certain. She still had to reach the dock on level four and somehow find a way onto a ship. And the longer she spent in this place, the more likely it was they would be discovered and recaptured. With five pairs of feet creeping around instead of just her own, achieving a stealthy getaway would be almost impossible. She knew her best chance was to go now, and go it alone. However, she also knew that if she survived, her conscience would eat at her for the rest of her life.

"What's your name?" Liberty asked, turning back to the man.

"Tobin, my name is Tobin Rand," said the man. "I was kidnapped by the Council for ransom. My mother runs a large shipping corporation out of Tharsis City on Mars."

Liberty cocked an eyebrow at him, "Not the Jewel Star Liner company, by any chance?"

Tobin shook his head, "No, but I think they're one of our subsidiaries." Then he shrugged, "Only, we own so many things it's hard to keep track."

Liberty smiled, "Tobin, you've just become my favorite person."

"Honestly, I can't keep up with it all," Tobin continued, seemingly forgetting they were standing in what was essentially a jail, with armed men outside the door. "Mom is trying to groom me to take over the business, but it all bores the crap out of me, to be honest."

Liberty shook her head. Why this guy was choosing that moment to tell her his life story was beyond her. "Look, that's really fascinating and all, but we need to move," said Liberty, handing him the skelly. "Rest this on the lock on the far cage, while I try to open the center one."

Tobin nodded, and then took the device. "So, what's your plan to get away?"

Liberty shrugged, "Get to the dock on level four, without getting killed."

Tobin's eyes widened, but Liberty just gave him a gentle nudge in the direction of the cell. "We'll figure it out on the way, just hurry."

Tobin nodded and turned towards the cell at the far end, but then froze. Blocking his path was the body of the man that Werner's guard had mown down earlier. Liberty glanced down at the body, also having forgotten it was there, and then looked away. The sight of it made her stomach churn, but the sensation was driven by fear, rather than revulsion.

"Hey, we can't help him," said Liberty, looking back at Tobin, whose face had drained of blood. "But we can save the others, if we act fast. So, clear your head and focus, and we'll all get out of here alive."

Tobin nodded and ran off, taking a wide path around the dead body. Liberty blew out a sigh, grateful that her motivational speech had worked on Tobin. She just wished it'd had the same effect on herself.

Liberty quickly began to scout the room for anything she could use to break open the middle cell. Not having to wait for the skelly to decode two more locks might only save a couple of minutes, but she knew that could be the difference between escape and recapture.

She tried the doors on the windowless rooms, but all were locked, except for one. She pulled it open and stepped inside, but then froze. There was a single chair in the center of the room, stained red with blood, with a drain on the floor directly beneath it. Other than the chair, there was a table, on top of which were a number of tools. Liberty cautiously stepped closer and then to her horror realized they were also stained red in places. *These aren't tools; this is a damned torture chamber!* She realized.

Shaking off the disgust at what she'd discovered, Liberty grabbed a blood-stained crowbar from the table, hoping she might be able to use it to pry open the lock's service panel. She was about to leave when she spotted another weapon, except this was something she was much more familiar with. She grabbed the pair of tonfa and slid them through her belt, hoping it wouldn't be necessary to use them, and ran back outside.

She was about to sprint back to the cells, when she heard the lock click on the door to Werner's office. It opened, and the guard who had put her in the cell earlier stepped in, accompanied by a second guard. They were busy chatting and laughing, and didn't immediately notice Liberty. However, as the second guard closed the door and both took a few steps towards the cells, they finally spotted Liberty, and their expressions hardened.

Liberty had the element of surprise and she used it, throwing the crowbar at the closest guard, then racing towards them. The crowbar struck the guard's collar bone, and he jolted back, crying out in agony. Fortunately for Liberty, the stricken guard collided into his companion, buying her the precious extra seconds she needed. Drawing the tonfa from her belt, Liberty parried the guard's flailing attempt to club her with the stock of his

SMG, and then spun the tonfa into his face. The guard stumbled back, but Liberty pressed her attack, punching the end of the tonfa into his chest, then striking him across the temple. The guard went down, but Liberty saw the second try to raise his SMG. However, with a cracked collarbone, the man was struggling to hold the weapon with any stability. Liberty switched grips on the tonfa, hooking the guard's machine gun and dragging it down, before hammering the end of the second tonfa into the bridge of his nose.

The fight was over in a matter of seconds, leaving Liberty breathless and shaky. It was only now that the pain in her thigh started to shoot through her body again. She took the weight off her injured leg. Whether due to adrenalin or the healing accelerants, it was starting to feel much stronger. Then she saw Tobin coming back towards her, with the two people from the end cell. Reaching down, she quickly searched the guard, removing his key fob and throwing it to Tobin.

"Use that to unlock the middle cell," Liberty called over. "And then try to find us another way out of here."

Tobin nodded, glancing anxiously at the two unconscious guards, before grabbing the ID fob and running back to the cells. Liberty moved to the second guard and removed his key fob. She then recovered the crowbar that she'd flung at the guard from where it had fallen to rest on the deck. "I hope this works..." she said out loud, running to the door to Werner's office. She rammed the crowbar underneath the bottom of the door, hoping it would act as a wedge, and delay anyone else from coming through.

Liberty turned back and saw Tobin waving her over. Still breathless, and muscles burning from exertion and nervous energy, she sprinted over to him. "What have you found?" she asked, briefly meeting the terrified, but hopeful eyes of the three other prisoners.

Tobin pointed to a shutter, low on the wall to their side. "This is a trash chute that runs down to level six. We can use it to get out."

"A trash chute?" said Liberty, unable to hide her disdain. She was beginning to think that fighting their way out through Werner's office was a preferable option.

"They don't put actual trash down it," said a young woman in dirty and torn clothing. She had been one of the prisoners in the far-right cell.

"Then what goes in there?" asked Liberty, though she was hesitant to learn the answer.

The woman forced down a dry swallow, then simply replied, "Bodies."

Liberty's eyebrows raced upwards and she looked back at Tobin, but he just shrugged, "I don't see that we have much of a choice."

There was the sound of banging from the far end of the room. Someone was trying to force their way through the door Liberty had wedged shut. She looked back at Tobin, then held open the door to the chute. "Seeing as this is your brilliant idea, you can go first..."

CHAPTER 26

The dock master watched Hudson and Morphus return from the adjacent hangar, and his eyes grew wide. It was either the surprise of seeing them still alive, or the sight of Morphus' shimmering body, or both, but he was clearly in shock.

"Release the docking clamps, we're leaving," Hudson called over to the dock master, which only seemed to make him more agitated.

"No, no, you can't!" he said, scurrying out from behind his counter. "The station is on security lock-down." He anxiously peered along the arched corridor that led onto the main concourse. "It's going crazy out there. They're looking for someone. The Council, I mean."

Hudson glanced at Morphus, "Our new friends in the other hangar must have been more important than we realized."

Morphus suddenly flickered, transforming into one of its previous male identities. It then flickered again, and switched back to the woman that Hudson was getting more used to seeing. There was an audible gulp from the dock master.

"The damage to my systems is more extensive than I first thought," said Morphus. "I must return to where I was created, at the Corporeals' homeworld. There, I can repair myself fully."

"I'll come with you," Hudson began, but Morphus shook its head.

"There is no need," Morphus replied. "My ship will sustain my systems for long enough to reach the Revocater facility. You must continue the search for the Liberty Devan entity, and for the crystal."

Hudson turned back to the dock master, "I need those clamps released. Make it happen!"

"I can't!" protested the dock master. "I can't override the security lockdown; it's out of my control."

Morphus leaned against the counter and rested its palm on the dock master's datapad. The alien's hand turned metallic and began to shimmer, and a second later the device lit up. Data cycled across its screen, too fast for Hudson to read, then a succession of powerful thuds rippled across the length of the docking bay.

"The docking clamps in this bay are all now released," Morphus said. "I have also enabled the docking ramps and airlock pods."

"But... how?" asked the dock master, staring at Morphus' shimmering hand as if it was a tarantula, creeping towards him. "What are you?"

"I am French," said Morphus, completely deadpan, and Hudson winced. "I will get the ships ready to launch," Morphus continued, turning to Hudson. "When we are free of this station, I will detach and return to the Corporeals' homeworld."

"Okay, you go. I'll be there in a minute," said Hudson, glancing down at the dock master's datapad, which now appeared to be fully unlocked. "I need to check on something first."

Morphus nodded and turned to leave, but then Hudson called out to it to stop. "Wait, how will we find each other again?"

"Your vessel was augmented with Revocater technology when I repaired it," said Morphus. "I will be able to track it, and find you."

Hudson acknowledged the alien, then watched as Morphus walked back to their conjoined vessels. Far from the agile and fluid movements Hudson was used to seeing, the entity was now walking like a geriatric. He didn't know if the being felt pain or fear, but it didn't matter to him. The deep uneasiness Hudson felt at seeing Morphus in distress was difficult to bear. And the fact it had sustained the injuries while saving him made it even harder to swallow.

"Who are you people?" asked the dock master, startling Hudson. "What was that thing?"

Hudson ignored the questions and grabbed the datapad on the counter.

"Hey, you can't look at that!" the dock master complained, trying to wrestle the device back off Hudson. However, Hudson's patience had worn thin. He grabbed the dock master's collar, and hauled him onto the counter top.

"I'm someone you don't want to piss off, right now," growled Hudson. It was like he'd switched to his tough guy relic-hunter persona, except this time he wasn't pretending. Then he pointed through the darkened archway into the adjacent hangar. "If you want to know what happens to people who piss me off, go and take a look in the next room."

The dock master's trembling eyes flicked over to the archway, then back to Hudson. Releasing his grasp on his collar, the dock master's feet slid back to the deck. He made no further complaints.

"The people that the Council traffic through this station, where do they end up?" Hudson asked, as a security guard entered the docking bay and started to look around.

"I honestly don't know," said the dock master. "All over the place. I only know that some ship's captains manage to smuggle a few to safety. But not many are willing risk it; if they get caught, they end up dead."

"Which captains?" said Hudson, finally feeling encouraged that he was getting somewhere. "And where do they take them?"

"Look, I already told you I don't know!" complained the dock master. "Some of the ships arrive from MP space; that's as much as I can tell you." Then he pointed to the datapad, "All the ships' movements are in there. Take it! Maybe you'll find something."

Hudson slipped the datapad into his jacket pocket, watching the security guard out of the corner of his eye. The guard seemed to be walking in his direction. Turning sharply, he started heading back towards the Orion, but then he heard a voice calling out.

"Hey, you, stop right there!" the guard yelled. "The station is on lock-down, didn't you listen?"

Hudson turned around, "Sure, but I'm just going to wait this out on my ship. Besides, it's not like I can go anywhere with the bay locked down."

The guard stepped closer. "What's that you put in your jacket?"

Hudson shrugged, "What's what?"

"Don't get smart, asshole," the guard said, now placing his hand on the grip of his sidearm. "I saw you take something off that counter. Now open your jacket, slowly, and take it out."

Hudson sighed, and slowly began to open his leather jacket. However, as he did so, he saw a figure crawling out from the archway leading to the second hangar. It was the heavy-set thug he'd clubbed with his pistol earlier.

"Stop him!" the man shouted. His voice was hoarse and croaky, but it still carried across the hangar.

The guard's head turned on a swivel. He saw the suited thug on the deck, then spun back to Hudson, drawing his weapon. However, Hudson had already reacted, stepping in and driving a thumping right cross into the guard's jaw. The man toppled over, knocked clean out in one hit.

"Don't tell me... I'm under arrest," Hudson said, shaking his throbbing hand. Then he saw more guards gathering outside in the concourse, and he knew he had to move fast. He didn't want to leave without Liberty, but the truth was he had no idea if she was even on the station. And after his brief visit, he doubted he'd ever be let back on again. He wasn't giving up, but he needed to find another way to reach her. And maybe the datapad in his pocket would provide the answers.

Hudson turned away from the commotion out in the concourse, and trudged up the rear ramp into the Orion. He felt deflated, but he was far from defeated. Somehow, he'd find Liberty again. He had to, because he didn't know what he would do without her.

CHAPTER 27

The garbage chute unceremoniously spat Liberty out into a waiting commercial refuse bin. She landed heavily and groaned, brushing some unidentified grime off her jacket. It had been a nightmarish helter-skelter ride, but Liberty was at least grateful that she hadn't come to rest on top of a dead body.

Tobin helped her out of the bin, and she looked around their new location. It certainly appeared to be a garbage processing facility, though Liberty shuddered to think what actually burned inside the furnace in the far corner.

"This refuse processing facility is on level six," said Tobin. "If we head out onto the main concourse, we can ride the travellator all the way down to level four."

Liberty shook her head and pointed to the two disheveled figures in rags. They were a few meters away, and still looked shell-shocked. "We won't get far with those two dressed like that," said Liberty. "We need to find them some other clothes, so that they blend in a bit more."

Tobin stroked the smooth skin on his chin and indicated towards the office. "Maybe we can find some coveralls in there, or in one of the other rooms?"

"Worth a try, why don't you check it out, while I talk to the others?" shrugged Liberty. Then she scowled, and eyed Tobin more suspiciously. "You seem remarkably calm, considering everything."

"It's not the first time I've been kidnapped for ransom," Tobin replied. "But it is the first time I've ever escaped. They won't kill me, though; I'm worth too much alive."

"How nice for you," Liberty said, sarcastically. "So, what's a rich kid doing on a dump like New Providence?" Given the sorts of debauched activities the station seemed famous for, Liberty was eager for an explanation. If Tobin was here for the same reason as most others had been, her opinion of the young man would take a sharp nose-dive.

Tobin smiled and threw his hands out wide, "Looking for adventure of course!"

Liberty wasn't amused, "This isn't a joke, Tobin," she snapped. "A rich kid like you might have a whale of a time in the casinos and brothels, but most people here aren't so lucky."

Tobin seemed offended, "Hey, I'm not like that," he protested. "I was just hoping to find a merc or hunter that would come with me out to the fringe planets. I wanted to see the edge of known space, you know? The final frontier. I hate this crappy station as much as you do."

Liberty sighed, though she was a little buoyed by Tobin's response. Yet he was still acting like he was in a video game with multiple lives, and she needed him to sober up, fast. "Look Tobin, you might be worth more alive than dead, but the rest of us aren't. For the rest of us, this is life and death."

Tobin nodded and looked much more somber, "Sure, I'm sorry, I wasn't thinking."

Liberty took a deep breath. As much as Tobin's privilege irked her, she needed him. "You were thinking well enough to get us down here. Now, find those two some clothes, and think how we can get to level four, without getting caught."

Tobin nodded again and moved away. Liberty suddenly became aware that the others had been watching and listening.

"What happens now?" asked the young woman in rags who had pointed out the macabre use of the trash chute earlier.

Liberty walked up to them. Somehow, she had inadvertently become the leader of their little escape party. She was way out of her comfort zone, but she also realized she had no choice but to accept the role that had fallen to her.

"What are your names?" Liberty asked, looking at the young woman in rags first.

"Pearl," said the woman, "and this is my brother, "Kris."

Liberty then looked to the man who had been in the middle cell. He was older, perhaps similar in age to Liberty, and wearing work overalls.

"I'm Jonas," he said, sounding a little less rattled than the other two. "Thanks for getting me out of there. I was afraid I was going to end up like Charlie. He was the guy they... you know..."

"I remember," said Liberty, cutting him off. Seeing the man he'd identified as Charlie getting brutally gunned down would be something she'd never be able to forget.

"Look, I'd love to tell you I have a plan for getting out of here, but the truth is, I'm making this up as we go along." Liberty saw the heads of Pearl and Kris drop, and so was quick to add, "But, Tobin – the rich kid in the suit – is well connected. If we can get to the dock on level four, he can get us on a ship off this crap heap."

Tobin came running out of the office with two sets of coveralls. He slung one each to Pearl and Kris. "Sorry if they don't fit great, but it's the best I could find."

"Okay, so the plan is that we move out and head to the main concourse," said Liberty, as Pearl and Kris pulled the coveralls on over their tattered clothes. "Try to act normal, so don't rush, or look anyone else in the eye," Liberty went on. "Take the travellators down to level four, and head for the dock. We're looking for a Jewel Star Liners freighter or transport ship. Everyone understand?"

The others all nodded, and Liberty turned back to Tobin, shifting the tonfas around to her back, so they looked less conspicuous.

"You're pretty good with those," said Tobin, pointing to the weapons. "And you're pretty good at that too. Motivational speeches, I mean. My mom would like you."

Liberty frowned. She wasn't sure if that was intended as genuine praise, or if it was some wildly misjudged attempt to hit on her. "Erm, thanks," she said, still frowning. "Now, come on rich kid, since you know this hell hole better than I do, lead the way."

Tobin led them to the exit and pulled open the door just enough for Liberty to peek through. It led into what appeared to be an office space, which Liberty assumed was probably the administrative section of the facility.

"Alright, rich kid, seeing as you're dressed for the part, walk out there like you own the place," said Liberty turning back to Tobin. "We'll slip straight through, acting like everything is normal."

Tobin looked at the sign on the wall, which said, 'Rectekk Waste and Recycling', and raised his eyebrows. "You know, I might *actually* own this place."

Liberty rolled her eyes, "Well, this should be no trouble for you then..." Turning to the others, she added, "Heads up, eyes forward, everyone. Just follow Tobin and act like we're supposed to be there."

Liberty took a deep breath, and opened the door fully, following Tobin as he strutted ahead, chest puffed out. Confused eyes followed them from behind computer monitors, but initially no-one spoke up. Then a smartly-dressed woman at a corner desk rose and blocked Tobin's path.

"Excuse me, just who the hell are you?" she said, immediately going on the offensive.

"Just keep walking..." Liberty muttered to Tobin from behind.

"How dare you, I am Tobin Rand!" said Tobin, indignantly, while brushing past the woman and continuing towards the door. "My associates and I have just completed the inspection of your facility. Terrible! Now, out of my way, before I include your name in my report to the owners!"

Liberty smiled vacantly at the woman and scuttled ahead, pulling open the door that led onto the corridor outside. "After you, sir..." she said to Tobin, who made a swift exit, followed by Jonas, Pearl and Kris, practically at a jog.

"Report me to the owners? I *am* the owner!" the woman snarled.

Liberty saw Tobin's face fall, but he recovered well, "Oh, well, in that case, expect my report in the morning!" he called back from the corridor outside. Then Tobin gave a short bow, before slipping out of sight along the corridor. Liberty smiled again at the woman, whose face was red and looked like it was about to explode. "Good afternoon," she said, trying to mimic Tobin's genteel accent, before stepping outside and closing the door swiftly behind her.

"Well that went well," said Liberty, catching up to Tobin and the others. Though the young man looked like he was ready to have a heart attack. "Which way do we go now?"

Tobin quickly got his bearings then pointed to an intersection ahead. "We head down there and then swing left on the main concourse. The travellator is in the center; you can't miss it."

Liberty took the lead, walking at a brisk pace. However, she resisted the urge to run, conscious of the need to remain inconspicuous. On a station like New Providence, if you were running, there was a good chance you were running away from something, or someone. Thankfully, there was plenty of foot fall outside and they all blended into the crowd seamlessly. Turning left onto the main concourse, Liberty saw the large, six-lane travellator, leading to the levels above and below, and felt a flicker of hope. However, she had barely taken a step towards it, when the public address system chimed an announcement.

"This is a security lock-down. Wanted fugitives are loose on the station," the booming voice of the announcer began.

A group of people next to Liberty laughed as this played. "Who isn't a wanted fugitive on this shithole?" said one of the men, and the others all laughed along with him.

Then every single infopanel on the station switched to show pictures of Liberty and Tobin. These quickly cycled to mug shots of Jonas, Pearl and Kris.

"If you see these fugitives, report them immediately to the security forces on the station," the guttural announcer continued.

Liberty's eyes widened, and she glanced over at the man next to her. His eyes moved from the infopanels down to Liberty. She placed her hand around the handle of one of her tonfa, expecting a fight, but the man simply held up his hands.

"Hey, lady, they didn't mention a reward for handing you in, so I don't give a shit what you did, or why they want you."

Liberty laughed, and turned to Tobias. "You have to love mercenary thinking."

"Actually, it makes a nice change not to have a bounty on my head," said Tobias. "Not that I'm complaining. Come on, we need to move quickly."

Liberty set off at a jog, figuring there was little point trying to remain inconspicuous with all of their faces blown up six-feet high on a hundred infopanels. She reached the top of the travellator, suddenly conscious that everyone was giving her a wide berth, but then she froze. Two security guards were bustling past the travelers on the opposite walkway, working their way up.

Liberty took a deep breath, and committed herself. Drawing the tonfas from her belt and holding them in the natural grip, so that the shafts rested across her forearms, she charged at the guards. Pain shot through her thigh, but the sudden burst of speed was enough to take the guards completely by surprise. She ploughed through the center of the two men, driving the tonfas into their throats, before they'd even realized she was coming. Liberty's leg then gave way, and she tumbled down to the bottom of the travellator like a ragdoll. For a few seconds, she just lay, sprawled out on the deck, paralyzed by exhaustion and pain. Then she felt hands grabbing underneath her arms, hauling her up.

"You're one crazy lady, do you know that?" said Tobin, smiling at her.

"Don't say your mom would like me, or I'll use these on you next," said Liberty, raising the tonfas.

Tobin laughed, "Well, she would," he said, but then quickly changed the subject. "We're almost there; just one more level down and dock four is directly to our left."

Tobin led the group as Liberty struggled to keep up the pace, due to the shooting pain in her thigh.

She glanced behind, and saw three more guards at the top of the travellator, scouring the crowds looking for them. *This is going to be close...* she thought.

Liberty reached the second travellator and pushed through the pain barrier to catch up with the others. Tobin reached the bottom first, and urged Jonas on, slapping his back as he ran past. Pearl and Kris were next, but as they reached the foot of the moving walkway, Liberty heard a shot ring out. Pearl fell, and then Kris dropped to her side, screaming. Blood coated his hand as he pressed it over the wound to his sister's side.

Liberty peered past them, looking for the shooter, as the crowd scattered in all directions, like startled pigeons. Then on her left she saw two security guards moving up towards Tobin, yelling at him to put up his hands. Liberty ducked down behind the side barrier of the travellator. She hadn't yet reached the bottom, and the guards hadn't spotted her.

Tobin and Jonas shot their hands up in the air as the guards approached. Liberty bided her time, sucking in deep breaths, waiting for the perfect moment to strike. A few meters from the bottom, she used the momentum of the moving walkway and raced forwards, swinging the first tonfa into the closest guard's throat, before punching him with the second. The other guard reacted more quickly than Liberty had expected, shifting his aim towards her, but Tobin managed to grab the guard's arm, deflecting his aim. A shot rang out, but it flew wild, and Liberty seized the opportunity to attack. She thrust the head of the tonfa into the guard's sternum, before whipping the second across the side of his head, sending him down hard.

Lungs burning, Liberty turned back to Pearl. Kris was still at her side, pressing his hands over the wound. Blood was leaking from the hole, but the young woman was still alive. Moving her was the last thing Liberty wanted to do, but she had no choice. If they left Pearl on the deck, she'd certainly die.

"We have to carry her!" Liberty cried, looking at Tobin and Jonas. "Grab under her shoulders and her legs."

Liberty ran ahead, through the archway into docking bay four. She then darted over to the dock master's counter, startling the man cowering behind it.

"Jewel Star Liners, where are they?" Liberty called out to the man. "Quickly, we need to get off this station!"

The dock master glanced at Liberty, recognizing her at once. "You're the one they're looking for!" he said, "You have to get out of here! If they find you, they'll think I had something to do with it."

Liberty aimed a tonfa at him, "Look, mister, if you don't help me, I'll definitely tell them you were helping me to escape."

"But, wait..." the dock master stammered, though Liberty was not giving way.

"Jewel Star Liners! Which bay?!"

The man pointed over to the far corner, "Bay six, but the station is on lock down. The captain won't leave, they'll just intercept him and destroy his ship."

Liberty shut her eyes and sighed; she hadn't considered that possibility. However, she knew that if they stayed, they'd be captured or killed, anyway. She didn't see that she had a choice. "I'll take that chance," said Liberty. She glanced over to the archway and saw that Tobin and the others had just entered.

"Bay six, go!" Liberty called over to Tobin. Then she had an idea. Turning back to the dock master, she asked, "Can you seal that archway? There must be an emergency door, in case the docking bay loses pressure or something like that?"

"There's a manual control by the side of the arch," the dock master replied. "But access is restricted. You need the master ID fob."

Liberty glanced down at the man's belt. "You mean that one?" she said pointing the tonfa at the collection of ID fobs he was wearing.

The man winced, as he realized the painful stupidity of his mistake. "Please don't make me give you this..." he said.

Liberty rested the two tonfa on the counter, and then locked eyes with the man. "Then don't make me make you..."

The dock master groaned and removed the bundle of ID fobs, throwing it onto the counter.

"Do me at least one favor," the dock master said, as Liberty grabbed the set of ID fobs. "Knock me out or something so it at least looks like I resisted."

Liberty moved around the side of the counter, as urgent voices grew louder in the concourse. She held the tonfa ready, and nodded at the dock master, who closed his eyes.

"Will it hurt?" the man said, eyes still shut tight.

Liberty spun out the weapon, striking him across the side of his head. He crumbled to the deck, but Liberty managed to partially catch him, and break his fall. "Yes," she said, as she rested him flat on his back. "It'll hurt like hell..."

Rushing back to the archway, she saw five security guards gathering on the concourse. She yanked open the emergency panel and began to cycle through the key fobs, pressing each one to the lock. For the first one the light turned red. *Damn it, come on!* Liberty urged, glancing back through the archway. The guards were on their way; she had only seconds to close the door. She pressed the second fob to the lock and waited.

Another red light. Third fob... red light again. "Come on!" she yelled out loud, pressing the fourth fob to the lock. The wait was agonizing, but then the light turned green, and the inner panel opened. Liberty grabbed the handle and yanked it down, causing the emergency door to slam shut like the blade of a guillotine. She rested her head against the metal of the archway, feeling about ready to collapse. However, they weren't in the clear yet.

Rushing over to bay six, she found Tobin arguing with the captain of a Jewel Star Liner ship.

"Look, I don't give a shit if you're Vespa Rand's son," the captain was saying, "You could be the King of England for all I care, I'm not leaving. The Council run this place, and they'll gun us down before we get even half-way to the portal!"

Liberty stepped up, "If you take us, he'll make sure you get paid two years' salary as a bonus."

The captain and Tobin both looked at her, mouths agape. "What?" Liberty shrugged, "You're good for it, right, rich kid?"

"Well, yeah..." said Tobin, also shrugging. "I guess I am."

The captain's eyes narrowed, "Make it three years' salary, and you have a deal."

"Captain, if you get us to Mars in one piece, I'll pay you four years' salary, and hand it to you on a silver platter," said Tobin.

The captain's narrowed eyes suddenly widened again. He stroked his fingers across his chin, then said, "Bollocks, I'm going to regret this, but what the hell, get on board..."

CHAPTER 28

The Orion cleared the dock and Hudson engaged the main drives, putting some welcome distance between himself and New Providence station. He wouldn't be sorry to see the back of OPW space, but it was still gut-wrenching to be leaving without Liberty. Despite knowing there was nothing more he could have done, he felt like he'd failed her again.

The communications panel blinked and Hudson opened the channel to Morphus' ship.

"I will detach now and begin my journey to the Corporeal's homeworld," said Morphus.

"Understood," replied Hudson. "How are you feeling?"

There was a pause, before Morphus answered. "My base functions are still severely impaired." Then with a much more human touch, it added, "But I feel fine, thank you."

"Then I'll see you when you get back," said Hudson. "Good luck."

"I wish you success also," replied Morphus. "I will return as expediently as circumstances allow." Then the channel clicked off, and Hudson felt a solid kick against the Orion's hull as the alien vessel detached. A few seconds later, Morphus' ship powered out in front of him, and vanished into the starry blackness at astonishing speed.

The navigation scanner bleeped, and Hudson checked it, noting that three new contacts had just appeared. He checked the registry IDs of each vessel. One of the ships was a Jewel Star Liners transport, on course towards the portal. It was a common, mid-sized commercial space liner, and ordinarily Hudson would have paid it no attention. However, he recalled the dock master saying that the station was on lock-down. Unless that status had changed, this lone transport shouldn't have been able to depart.

He parked this thought for a moment, and checked the registry information for the other two ships, but they came up blank. Hudson could see that they were both XJ-11 Assault Gunboats, a type of light attack vessel that the MP military phased out and sold off a decade ago. It offered no creature comforts, like the RGF Patrol Crafts, but it was similarly agile and capable in combat situations. It was the perfect short-range vessel for mercenaries or private security forces. And with blank registry IDs, their actions would be almost impossible to link back to them, or to any particular organization. *The Council...* Hudson realized. *Looks like I pissed them off pretty badly...*

Hudson angled the nose of the Orion towards the portal and began to accelerate, while watching the scanner closely. However, instead of both gunboats turning towards the Orion, as Hudson expected, one had set an intercept course for the liner instead.

"What are you up to?" muttered Hudson, watching the chevron on the scanner. The liner then put on a sudden burst of acceleration, clearly trying to make a run for it. However, Hudson had flown that type of liner before, and knew its capabilities well. They were built like tanks, and moved about as fast. There was simply no chance it could outrun the gunboat.

The communications panel flashed again and Hudson sighed. The Jewel Star Liner had just put out a mayday. With the station on lock-down, there were no other ships in the vicinity, not that he would have expected any of them to answer the mayday. The only other vessel nearby was the Orion, which meant that Hudson was faced with another hard choice.

Hudson checked his distance to the portal again. If he continued at his current rate, he'd be able to jump long before the gunboat could close to weapons range. He also knew he'd be jumping away in the full knowledge that the liner would either be captured or more likely destroyed. The smart, albeit callous option, was to go anyway. The priority, even above that of rescuing Liberty, was to find Cutler and Griff, and recover the crystal. He couldn't do that if he was blown to pieces by the hired guns of angry Council mobsters. He knew that he should continue his run for the portal. He also knew that he wouldn't be able to live with himself if he did.

Hudson throttled back the main engines and spun the Orion one hundred and eighty degrees. Clenching up tight, he then slammed the throttle forward again, initiating a three-g burn, which began to sharply reduce his velocity towards the portal. As the Orion slowed, the closing velocity of the other ships increased. It was like playing a game of chicken, except at thousands of kilometers per hour.

The gunboat clearly wasn't in a mood for games. Hudson's last-second, crazy change of course had caused it to veer away dramatically. Hudson saw tracer rounds fly off harmlessly into space above him. *Panic flying and panic shooting... the Council needs to find itself some better pilots,* Hudson thought.

Hudson then watched the smaller gunboat burn hard in an attempt to match the Orion's relative velocity. However, Hudson was already tracking its position, and pushing the Orion even harder to close the distance. All the gunboat had achieved was to give Hudson the advantage. He flipped a switch on his instrument panel, and the whir of the Orion's weapon systems deploying rattled through the deck. Hudson locked onto the engines of the target vessel and prepared to fire. One shot from the main cannon would obliterate the small attack craft. However, as much as the Council ship probably deserved to burn in space, Hudson wasn't about to gun it down in cold blood.

The gunboat appeared to recognize the danger it had put itself in, and tried to run, but with the augmentations that Morphus had made, the Orion was significantly faster and more agile. Hudson waited for the little ship to fill the targeting reticle, then he squeezed the trigger.

The ventral cannon rattled off a volley of rounds, pulverizing the gunboat's single main drive. The ship went into an uncontrolled spin, with electrical arcs erupting from its aft section, like a sparkler being waved on Independence Day.

Hudson adjusted course again to intercept the second gunboat, but it was already almost on top of the liner. He opened a channel to the vessel, hoping it had just seen what had happened to its companion.

"Unregistered gunboat, break off your pursuit," Hudson demanded. His previous victory had given him confidence, and he sounded clear and assertive, but there was no response from the gunboat. Hudson stayed calm and made constant micro-adjustments to his course, leading the target as the gunboat continued to charge down the liner.

"Unregistered gunboat, I say again, break off your pursuit," Hudson repeated. "I am responding to a mayday. I will act in defense of this vessel, unless you discontinue your pursuit immediately."

There was still no response. *Come on, damn it, give up!* Hudson urged. Then the gunboat suddenly cut its engines, and pulsed its thrusters, lining up the cannons on its wing tips with the Orion instead.

"Shit!" Hudson shouted, changing course, but the gunboat had already got a shot off. Hudson felt the ship shudder, and a red light flashed up on his damage control panel. He didn't look at it. The gunboat and liner raced past, and Hudson fought the controls to bring the Orion back in line with the target. The gunboat's maneuver had caused it to lose some ground to the liner, but Hudson too had been forced out of weapons range. With time running out, he adjusted his trajectory, flying purely by eye, and rammed the throttle hard forward.

The forces on his body increased to painful levels, but soon the gunboat crept back into range. He checked the ventral cannon, but the automatic targeting system was down, possibly as a result of the hit he'd taken. He'd have to use the nose cannon, which meant aiming the old-fashioned way.

"Mark-one eyeball it is then," said Hudson, making minute adjustments with the thrusters. He checked the relative distances again and saw that the gunboat was almost in range of the liner. It was now or never. He made one more tiny adjustment, leading the target like a World War Two Spitfire pilot, and fired. The cannon shells flew off ahead, and seconds later the gunboat exploded. Hudson quickly veered away to avoid the debris, then eased off the main drives, before releasing the controls. His hands ached and fingers throbbed, but the pain had been worth it. The liner was safe.

He blew out a long breath, then reached down to the communications panel to let the liner know they were out of danger. However, all the lights on the panel were red. "Shit, that little gunboat bastard must have hit my antenna array," said Hudson, flipping switches on and off, as if that might suddenly cause it to work again. "Where's Morphus, when you need it?" he added, glancing over to the second seat, which was empty once again. Though at this point he'd settle for any crappy repair station.

He let out another long sigh, and relaxed his aching muscles, but he'd barely closed his eyes before the navigation scanner bleeped again. Hudson groaned as he glanced down to see four more unregistered gunboats launching from New Providence.

"I think that's my cue to leave..." said Hudson, again directing the comment to the empty second seat. He was close to the portal now, so there was no chance of the gunboats catching him, or the liner. Though after what he'd just done, he knew he'd not get within a hundred kilometers of New Providence station again, at least not in the Orion. If Liberty was still there, she was on her own. Or she was already dead. Either way, Logan Griff and Cutler Wendell would pay for what they did. Even if Goliath succeeded in annihilating Earth, Hudson would make sure he got to Griff and Cutler first. Even if the galaxy was being torn down around him, Hudson would make sure he got his revenge.

CHAPTER 29

Logan Griff lifted the bulky scendar device containing the alien crystal onto the table, and slid it into the middle. He then flopped down into one of the waiting office chairs and lounged in it, like he was a bored schoolchild.

"Why the hell are we meeting in this cesspit of freaks and weirdos?" said Griff, as he ran a tired hand through his stringy hair. He had directed the question to Superintendent Jane Wash, who was sitting opposite. "Sapphire Alpha is nowhere near anything of value, and there are about a million nut-jobs on the planet living like it's the Middle Ages again."

Wash's thin lips pouted and she scowled, before letting out a loud, disappointed sigh at Griff. She reached forward and dragged the scendar device closer. Griff watched as Wash bent down to peer in at the crystal through the window, but she appeared utterly unimpressed by it.

"It's precisely because Sapphire Alpha is in the middle of nowhere that we're here," Wash said, in her usual condescending tone. She straightened her back again, resuming her stiff, upright posture. "This may be a backwards OPW planet, but it has the only space station in the entire system. It's an insignificant world in an insignificant star system that's practically undefended." Then she tapped the device with the tip of her manicured fingernail. "If you can find a portal and an alien wreck out here, then it will be easy to stake our claim. Conversely, if we discover a new portal closer to MP or CET space, we will face much sterner resistance."

"Smart..." replied Griff, yawning.

"One of us has to be," said Wash, tersely.

Griff reached into his top pocket and snuck out a cigarette from the squashed black packet that was tucked inside. He popped it into his mouth and lit it, before sucking in a deep lungful of smoke.

"Must you do that?" Wash complained. "This station reeks enough as it is."

Griff cocked his head back and blew the smoke away from where Wash was sitting. He knew better than to antagonize her any more than was necessary, though he enjoyed pushing her buttons for as long as he could get away with it. However, the truth was that he hadn't lit the smoke to annoy his commander; he'd needed it to soothe his nerves. Despite the great enjoyment he'd got from selling off Liberty Devan to the Council, other recent experiences had given him pause. Though he may have re-asserted his authority over Cutler Wendell, the once predictable mercenary had become more impulsive, and his control over Tory Bellona had waned. Combined with almost dying on an alien space station, and the edgy meeting he'd had with Werner on New Providence, he was feeling particularly brittle.

"I've had a stressful few days," Griff eventually said, in answer to Wash's snarky question. He blew out another plume of smoke then quickly got back on topic. "Even if I do find a portal and a new wreck, this is still OPW space. Won't they just say it's theirs?"

Wash rested back in her chair. "The Outer Portal Worlds are a loose union," she said, making a show of wafting the smoke away, even though barely any had gone near her. "So long as we stop any OPW colonization caravans from reaching the planet, they can't apply for the new world to join."

"And what about the CET and the MP?" asked Griff, before sucking in another lungful of smoke.

"Oh, I have no doubt that they will come," said Wash. She appeared unconcerned at the prospect of the two largest military powers descending on them. "But I already have a fleet of RGF Patrol craft standing by. Once you find a wreck, I'll send them in to blockade the portal. Neither will risk a conflict. They will have to accept our claim."

Griff took another long drag and blew out the smoke, again being careful to direct it away from Wash. Then he tapped the ash into a glass ashtray on the table and reclined back in the chair. "Well, it certainly seems like you've got it all figured out."

"It certainly seems like you've got it all figured out, *ma'am*," Wash answered, acidly. "Don't forget your place, Inspector Griff. I put you where you are. I can toss you out into the gutter just as easily."

The stern tone of his superior compelled Griff to sit up, as if to attention. He hated that Wash could still make him do that, like a dog being commanded to beg or roll over. He stubbed out his cigarette in the ashtray and cleared his throat, "My apologies, *ma'am*," he said, a little more cockily than he'd intended.

"You got the device, so for that you deserve some credit," Wash went on, before leaning in towards Griff. "But you're becoming sloppy. Sentimental."

Griff scowled as Wash stood up and marched around in front of him. She perched on the edge of the table, brushing the ashtray away, then peered down at him. Griff caught himself staring at Wash's ass, before forcing his eyes to meet hers.

"You were seen at New Providence, talking to the Council," Wash said. Her words were calm, and carefully measured, but Griff could tell she was angry. "Questions were asked further up the chain. Questions that could have shone a light on my plan, and implicated others. Others who are not as tolerant of failure as I am."

"I'm sorry, ma'am," Griff said. He hadn't even considered that his presence on New Providence might have been reported, or even observed at all. "I just had some business to deal with, that's all."

Wash laughed, then repeated Griff's words back to him, in a mocking tone. "I just had some business to deal with..." she said, as she slid off the table and sashayed back to her seat. Griff caught himself watching her ass again, but then felt dirty for doing it. "You should have killed Hudson Powell and the girl when you had the chance. Next time, I expect you not to fail."

"The girl won't be a problem anymore," said Griff, unable to prevent a smile from curling his lips. "And as for Powell, I'll deal with him soon enough."

"Make sure that you do," said Wash. Her tone sounded moderately less menacing now that she'd administered her verbal beating. She then pushed the scendar device back across the table to Griff. "Now, take this thing and find me a new portal and a fresh new alien wreck."

"Yes, ma'am," replied Griff, grateful that Wash had gone relatively easy on him for his detour to New Providence. He stood up and tucked the scendar under his arm, before heading for the door.

"Oh, and Inspector Griff," Wash called out, as Griff's hand landed on the door lever. He swallowed hard, and turned back to face her. "I expect my usual cut of the profits from the sale of Liberty Devan to the Council." Griff clenched his teeth, but said nothing. "And don't forget, you still owe me for Hudson Powell's quota. I expect you to make the transfer right away."

Griff pressed the handle down, adding so much pressure that it nearly snapped clean off. "Yes, ma'am," he said again, before pulling open the door and slamming it shut behind him.

CHAPTER 30

Tory Bellona brought the FS-31 patrol craft to a stop two hundred meters in front of the unopened portal. She released the controls and turned to Logan Griff. The RGF Inspector was standing behind Tory and Cutler in the cockpit, anxiously stroking his mustache.

"We're in position," said Tory. "Now let's see if your RGF goons actually knew what they were doing with that device."

Superintendent Jane Wash had brought a team of engineers with her to the station at Sapphire Alpha. The plan had been to install the scendar into Griff's ship, and have Cutler along as a defensive escort. However, the stripped back RGF Patrol Craft lacked the systems required to properly interface with the device; it had been fitted to Cutler's FS-31 instead.

Griff would have preferred not to have involved Cutler at all, given his recent misgivings about him. He'd tried to subtly suggest this to Wash, but she hadn't wanted to waste time trying to source another suitable vessel. And since Cutler was a known quantity, Wash had ordered Griff to proceed.

Ordinarily, Griff would have worried about the mercenary dispensing with the middle man, by killing him and stealing the device. However, with a dozen RGF Patrol Crafts on standby at Sapphire Alpha, even Cutler Wendell wouldn't be that audacious, or stupid.

"How about you stick to flying, and let me handle the complicated stuff?" Griff hit back at Tory, but the mercenary just laughed at him, and turned away.

Griff initiated the program that the RGF techs had installed in the computer, then stood back and peered out into space expectantly. Nervous seconds ticked by, but nothing happened. "Shit!" Griff swore, before confirming that the program was actually running. Everything checked out, but the portal still remained closed.

Tory laughed again, "Looks like it was a bit too complicated for them, not surprisingly."

"Why don't you just shut the hell up, Tory?!" Griff yelled at her, unable to keep a lid on his temper. His former soft spot for the mercenary was quickly developing a calloused skin.

Tory unclipped her harness and pushed herself out of the pilot's seat. "Why don't you make me, asshole?" she said, squaring off against Griff.

"Cutler, can you control your animal?" said Griff, directing the command at the second seat. However, Cutler appeared to be absorbed by the information on one of his monitors, and didn't respond.

"You're a real tough guy, aren't you, Logan Griff?" Tory went on, taking a step towards Griff and jabbing him in the chest with her finger. "It took real guts to lay into the Devan girl, when she couldn't fight back, right?"

"Cutler..." Griff said again, this time with more urgency. Again, Cutler ignored his plea.

"Then you bound her hands and traded her like cattle," Tory continued, shoving Griff back again, this time with the flat of her hand. "That must have made you feel really big, right? You pathetic piece of shit!"

Tory's hands balled into fists. Griff backed away again, but his back hit the rear bulkhead of the cockpit. "Cutler, damn it, call off your hound!"

"Liberty Devan has escaped from New Providence station," said Cutler Wendell, slowly turning his seat to face the others. The statement cut through the tension like a laser.

"What?" said Griff, sure that he'd misheard.

"My contact on New Providence just confirmed it," Cutler continued, pointing to the screen he'd been reading. "Liberty Devan escaped with four others aboard a Jewel Star Liners transport."

"That can't be right," Griff snarled, pushing past Tory and staring down at Cutler's monitor. He skim-read the contents quickly, but it was enough to confirm that what Cutler had said was true. "How is that even possible?" Griff yelled, pounding his fists on the console. "She was bound and locked up in a damn holding cell!"

"My contact says that a skelly was found," said Cutler, his eyes suddenly flicking to Tory. "Given that the girl was searched, before she was placed into the cell, the Council has concluded that someone smuggled her the device."

Griff threw his arms out wide, "Who the hell could have done that? She was with us for the entire time."

Cutler unclipped his harness and stood up, without taking his eyes off Tory. Griff noticed that his right hand was resting on the belt around his hip, just above where his sidearm was holstered. Then Griff glanced across at Tory. Her face was stony, and she made no move, but Griff had seen how quickly Tory could switch gears.

"Wait, you think Tory gave her the skelly?" said Griff. It seemed absurd that Tory would help Liberty Devan, but merely speaking the words out loud seemed to give life to the idea.

"Answer the question, Cutler," said Tory, without showing a flicker of emotion. She was practically daring him to accuse her directly.

Suddenly, Griff felt exposed. They were all in a cabin no more than four meters square, with only a thin layer of metal and glass separating them from the cold vacuum outside. A gunfight would end up killing them all, but the way Tory was looking at Cutler, Griff fully believed she was crazy enough to start one.

Griff's gaze flicked back to Cutler, waiting for him to respond. It felt like he hadn't taken a breath for a full minute.

"No, I do not believe you assisted her escape," said Cutler, in his usual, dry delivery. Griff finally let the air escape his lungs. However, while the answer may have prevented fists and bullets from flying, to Griff's ears, Cutler's answer had dripped with insincerity. And a quick glance back over to Tory suggested that she remained unconvinced too. Then Cutler turned to Griff, and added, "However, the Council will believe that we did."

Griff felt like he had dodged a bullet, only to step into the line of fire of another. "What does that mean?" he asked, though he was pretty sure that he already knew the answer. "You're saying that they'll be coming for us?"

"Almost certainly," answered Cutler, though his delivery still didn't betray any emotion.

"And there's no way to reason with them?" Griff went on, but Cutler merely shook his head.

Suddenly the lights in the cockpit dimmed and a panel on Cutler's console blinked rapidly. He bent over to check it, scowling.

"We are experiencing a significant power drain," Cutler called out, as the beat of the ship's reactor grew louder and faster. "The source is unknown."

In the gloom, Griff saw the device containing the alien crystal glowing brightly. "Wait a minute," he said, rushing over to the computer console where the RGF program had been running. "I'm getting something... A massive spatial distortion. Wait..."

Then the cockpit was suddenly drenched in a vivid purple light, forcing them all to turn away and bury their faces in their arms. Alarms rang out all around them, then suddenly silenced. The lights flickered back on, and the thrum of the FS-31's reactor resumed its normal cadence.

"Shit, it actually worked," said Griff, feeling a sudden rush of excitement. "The portal is open."

Cutler glanced at Tory, then returned to his seat to check his instruments. "Inspector Griff is correct; I am reading a portal directly ahead," said Cutler, while continuing to analyze the readings on his screen. "I suggest we move quickly. The portal opening sent out a tremendous amount of Shaak radiation. It will not be long before others detect the burst, and come looking."

"I'll let Wash know to send the patrol craft," said Griff, hurriedly tapping the message into the console. "But that radiation pulse is acting like a damn beacon. Every hunter in the area will have seen it." Griff turned to Tory, who had been the only one not to react to the news. "Well, are you going to fly us through, or not?"

Cutler also looked around, eagerly awaiting Tory's reaction, but she just shrugged. "What's the point?" she replied. "If the Council is going to hunt us down and kill us, we need to start looking out for ourselves. To hell with Jane Wash and the RGF."

"The Council may not listen to reason," said Griff, sitting down on the rear seat and fastening his harness. "But they understand the language of money. If there's an alien wreck on the planet that's through that portal, we get a percentage of every credit that's made at auction."

"You think you can buy Werner off?" sneered Tory. "And you had the nerve to call Hudson Powell dumb."

"They'll take the money," said Griff, shrugging off Tory's insult. "Because once we get done, we'll all be rich enough to buy our own private armies. We'll be untouchable."

Tory shook her head and shrugged again. "You're delusional," she laughed, "but, what the hell. it's not like I have anything better to do. And

I'd rather be on a portal world than stuck in here with your farting carcass."

Griff scowled at Tory, as she made her way back to the pilot's seat, then glanced across to Cutler. He was eyeing him suspiciously, but remained silent. Tory's basement-level opinion of Griff meant she was less likely to suspect his statement. It was just more bluster from someone she respected less than the dirt on her boots. Cutler, however, knew Griff was more devious than he appeared.

It was true that Griff only half-believed what he'd said to Tory. He knew it would take more than just credits to get the Council off their backs. If the Council believed that he, Cutler and Tory had double-crossed them, then Werner would make an example of them, to make sure no-one else was stupid enough to repeat their mistake. The only chance of stopping that from happening would be to hand Werner the culprit, along with a substantial amount of compensation. He suspected Cutler was probably thinking the same thing, and he hoped he also had the same fall guy – or more precisely, fall girl – in mind. It was something he planned to raise with the mercenary at the opportune moment. However, first they had to actually bag a big enough score to give them the capital they needed.

Tory engaged the engines, and then got up to recalibrate a number of secondary systems, in order to compensate for their earlier power drain.

However, before she sat down again, she stood in front of Griff, then leaned in close enough that her hair swung down and almost touched Griff's face. Despite everything that had happened and gone on between them, Griff couldn't help but feel slightly aroused. Then Tory spoke, and Griff's excitement was rapidly snuffed out.

"Oh, and by the way, Inspector Griff, you're not untouchable," said Tory. Her words were like poison being poured into his ear. "Not by me..."

CHAPTER 31

The waiter delicately placed a crystal tumbler onto the fine linen tablecloth. The deftness had been required because the tumbler was filled with what Tobin had described as, 'an obscene quantity of whiskey'. The waiter then picked up a champagne bottle from the ice cooler beside the table and topped up Tobin's crystal flute, before gracefully stepping away.

"Are you sure you don't want some of this?" asked Tobin, tapping his ornate glass, which chimed musically as he did so. "It's a pretty good vintage."

"I'm sure it is," replied Liberty, before taking a healthy gulp of the whiskey. She set the glass back down and tapped it, mimicking Tobin's earlier gesture. "But it won't kill as many brain cells as this stuff."

Tobin laughed, "And that's a good thing?"

"Probably not," admitted Liberty, smiling. "But it certainly takes the edge off, that's for sure." Then she looked out at the Martian landscape through the grand panoramic window of the restaurant, and sighed. "And this helps too," she said, gesturing to the rolling red hills and valleys. "I don't think I've eaten as well as this, and in such amazing surroundings, since... well, ever!"

"It's my pleasure," said Tobin, beaming back at her.

He was wearing an expensive-looking light-blue suit, which he had assured a disinterested Liberty was the latest fashion on Mars. Liberty was still wearing her relic hunter gear, though it had been patched up and cleaned, courtesy of the hotel's laundry service.

"We have cause to celebrate," Tobin continued. "We all escaped, and Pearl is going to make a full recovery."

"Thanks for footing the cost of her surgery," said Liberty. "You might be a spoilt little rich kid, but you're a half-decent kinda guy too."

"Gee, thanks," said Tobin, sarcastically. Then he raised his glass. "How about a toast?"

Liberty smiled and lifted her tumbler. "What shall we drink to?"

"How about, new friends?" said Tobin.

Liberty nodded, but then thoughts of Hudson flashed into her mind. She still didn't know whether he was alive or dead. Even with Tobin's influence and connections on Mars, he hadn't been able to locate VCX-110 M7070-Orion anywhere. She hadn't given up hope, though. Hudson was a survivor. She brought the tumbler closer to her lips, and said, "How about to new friends and friends lost, but not forgotten?"

Tobin acknowledged her with a short nod, and emptied the champagne flute in one, before letting out an exaggerated gasp of satisfaction.

Liberty laughed, "I should introduce you to Ma. If that's how you normally drink champagne, you'd make her a rich woman."

Tobin frowned, "Your mother owns a bar?"

"No, she's not my mom. Ma is short for Martina."

"So, what about your folks?" asked Tobin, a little tentatively. But when Liberty's face fell, he quickly added, "Hey, sorry, that was way too personal." Then he smirked and added, "Especially for a first date."

Liberty smiled again. "Don't push your luck," she said. "Besides, I'm half surprised you didn't invite your own mother to our little celebratory dinner."

"Ah, she's on business on Medusa Four," said Tobin, with a dismissive waft of his hand. "Or was it Zeus Two? Anyway, she's opening some new facility or whatever. Besides, I'm more interested to hear about this Martina character. Is she another relic hunter?"

"She was, but now she runs a place on Brahms Three. A safe place, and a good place if you like to drink hard."

The waiter returned and topped up Tobin's glass again. He thanked him, and took another healthy gulp. "I think I've had my fill of dangerous backwater planets. For the time being, at least."

Liberty was only vaguely paying attention to Tobin's answer. A small crowd of people had gathered around an infopanel behind the bar area.

"What's going on over there?" asked Liberty, nodding over to the bar.

Tobin looked over at the crowd and shrugged. "I have no idea. Why don't we go and find out?"

Liberty picked up her tumbler and wandered over with Tobin to get a closer look. It took a few moments to jostle into a position where she could see the screen, but then she realized what the excitement was about.

"Another new portal has been discovered," said Liberty. "Near a planet called Sapphire Alpha." Then she frowned, and looked at Tobin. "Where's that?"

Tobin thought for a moment, before answering, "It's a fringe world, I think. Technically, it's a member of the OPW, but it's an out-of-the-way, nothing place, really."

"Another backwater planet, huh?" said Liberty, referring to Tobin's jibe about Brahms Three. It didn't seem to register with him that Liberty had been affronted by his unkind description of the world. Since becoming a safe haven for the Orion, and for herself and Hudson, she'd developed more of an affection for the sweaty little planet.

"It's probably the most backwater of backwater planets," said Tobin, taking another slurp of vintage champagne.

Liberty turned her back on the crowd, and locked eyes with Tobin. This appeared to make him very nervous.

"What? What have I done?" he asked.

"Nothing, yet..." replied Liberty, cryptically. "But there is something I want you to do."

"Why do I get the feeling I'm not going to like it?" said Tobin, partially hiding behind his champagne flute.

"I want you to get me to Sapphire Alpha."

"Why the hell do you want to go there?" asked Tobin, almost spilling his champagne.

Liberty pulled him away from the crowd, and they sat back down at their table. "Look, the only way to find and open a new portal is with my scendar device."

"The thing those assholes who sold you to the Council stole?" asked Tobin. During their flight back to Mars, they'd had plenty of time to talk. Though Liberty had left out the part about the alien artificial intelligence, Morphus. She figured that little nugget of information might have been a bit too much to swallow, especially after their recent excitement.

"Yes, and that means that Cutler and Griff have opened that new portal," replied Liberty. "I have to get that device back. And, if Hudson is still alive, it's my best chance of finding him."

"You think he'd go after them too?" said Tobin.

Liberty nodded, "I know it."

Tobin blew out a heavy sigh, and rested back in his chair. "It's sounds pretty dangerous, Liberty. If you're caught..."

"I can take care of myself, Tobin," interrupted Liberty.

"Hey, I know that," said Tobin, sounding a little annoyed at being cut off. "But there are three of them, and only one of you."

"Look, can you get me to Sapphire Alpha or not?" Liberty wasn't interested in entertaining a conversation about how dangerous it was to go after Griff and the crystal. She was going, with or without his help. "With your fancy name, you can help charter a transport, or redirect a freighter or something, right?"

Tobin shook his head, "Even I don't have enough sway to redirect a ship way out there. Not any time soon, anyway."

Liberty sighed and downed what was left of the whisky in her tumbler. She placed the glass down and stared aimlessly out of the panoramic window.

"There has to be a way," she said out loud, but she was talking to herself, rather than to Tobin.

Tobin picked up Liberty's glass and waved it at the waiter, before placing it back on the table again. "There is *one* way," he said, making it sound like he was about to reveal a dirty little secret.

Liberty cocked her head, and glanced at him out of the corner of her eye. A streak of blue hair fell across her face. "That sounds ominous..."

"I may not be able to redirect a ship to Sapphire Alpha," Tobin went on, his expression adopting an air of mischief, "but I can take you there myself."

Liberty turned to face him. "You have a ship?"

Tobin smiled, "Benefits of being a rich kid, I suppose. It's a two-man personal shuttle. Luxury, of course."

"Of course," parroted Liberty.

"But it's comfortable, and it will get us to Sapphire Alpha, if you still want to go."

Liberty felt a rush of excitement; it seemed like the ideal solution. However, she then realized that she'd be putting Tobin in the line of fire, and her enthusiasm waned.

"It's a kind offer, but I'd be putting you in a lot of danger. You've already done enough."

It was now Tobin's turn to stare wistfully out at the Martian landscape. "I've not done a damn thing of value in my entire life," said Tobin. He sounded angry, but it was directed inward. "Helping to get you and the others off that station is the only worthwhile thing I've achieved." Then he met Liberty's eyes, and the playfulness that usually shone in them was replaced with a fresh resolve. "I want to help." Then he rested back in his chair again, and the roguish smirk returned. "Besides, if I don't get off Tharsis City before my mom gets back, she'll probably lock me in the condo, under armed guard."

Liberty laughed, "Penthouse suite, right?"

"Of course," replied Tobin.

The waiter brought over a fresh glass of whiskey, and placed it in front of Liberty. Before he left again, Liberty called out, "Wait, can you bring another, please?" The waiter nodded, and moved away.

"I've got my champagne, thanks very much," said Tobin, lifting his flute.

"If we're going to do this, then we need a proper drink to seal the deal," said Liberty, thinking back to her first moments with Hudson. "Captain's orders."

Tobin frowned, "How come you get to be captain when it's my ship?"

The waiter returned and placed the second glass of whiskey in front of Tobin, before again moving away.

"Because I call the shots," said Liberty, raising her tumbler. "I know these assholes better than you do. If you're coming along, you need to do as I say."

Tobin swapped his champagne flute for the tumbler of whiskey. He sniffed it and turned up his nose. "I hope that your choices as captain are more informed than your choice of drinks."

"So, do we have an agreement?" asked Liberty.

"You're the boss, Boss," said Tobin, raising his glass.

Liberty smiled, then downed the contents of her tumbler in one. She placed the empty glass down on the table and then looked at Tobin, expectantly. The young man blew out another sigh, then threw back the contents into his mouth. He swallowed hard, looking like he'd just eaten a thistle, then coughed and thumped his chest like a gorilla.

Liberty laughed, before reaching over and slapping his back. "I think you and I are going to make a great team."

CHAPTER 32

Hudson pressed his thumb to the credit scanner to pay the docking and repair fee at Deimos Station, and then strolled onto the corridor outside the hangar. He stopped, taking a look back at the Orion; the ship that had saved his ass more than once already. She was a fine companion, but she wasn't whole yet. She was still missing one of her crew.

He had managed to dock at Deimos without a swarm of MP military ships descending on him, thanks to his modified registry ID. The docking manifest had listed the ship under the ID, VCX-110 K2000-Shadow. However, it was still the Orion to Hudson.

Turning away from the docking hangar, he walked down the corridor and made a bee-line for The Winchester. It was early evening, Martian time, but Hudson wasn't tired. He'd been unable to stop his mind from fizzing with thoughts and ideas. He wondered how Morphus was, and where in the galaxy it was headed. He'd never thought to ask where the Corporeals' homeworld actually was. And he wondered about where Griff and Cutler had gone, and what they had planned for the scendar. Perhaps they had sold it off already, he mused.

Most of all he wondered where Liberty was, and if she was alright. It was this latter thought that had compelled him to head for The Winchester. He needed something to help him forget, if only for a moment.

He pushed in through the fake oak-paneled doors, and noted that the place had been given a minor face lift. There were a few new tables, and a fresh lick of paint, that still somehow seemed to look old. It had no doubt been funded by the hardbucks Liberty had unwillingly handed over, after their bar brawl.

The old-fashioned weapons hanging on the wall behind the bar remained, and they again made him think of Tory Bellona. However, he didn't want her in his head at that moment; not after she had been complicit in what happened to Liberty. That she'd seemingly again saved his own life on the alien world was secondary.

"I was wondering when you'd show your face again," said Roy the barman, as Hudson pulled up a stool at the bar. Roy then peered behind Hudson, with a concerned scowl on his face. "Where's your companion? She's not going to tear up my bar again, I hope? I just got it all fixed up."

"She's not with me at the moment," said Hudson, resting his elbows on the bar.

Roy's eyes widened slightly. He then reached below the counter and brought up a bottle of Bourbon and a single tumbler. "Want to talk about it?"

Hudson sighed and helped himself to a generous measure. Roy made no attempt to take the bottle away. "Not right now, thanks," he said, shooting a weak smile at the barman.

"Well, let me know when you do," said Roy, cheerfully. "I'll be here." Then he slid away to the other side of the bar to serve another customer, leaving Hudson alone. It had been some time, he realized, since he had drunk at a bar by himself. He hadn't minded being alone back then, but now he couldn't bear the feeling of emptiness.

He drank the first glass of Bourbon and then poured another. Then he pulled the datapad he'd taken from the dock master on New Providence out of his pocket, and slid it onto the bar. He'd already had time to check through its contents during the flight back to Deimos. Though if it contained evidence of ships' captains smuggling people off the station, he couldn't find it. And, if he was honest, that hadn't surprised him. It wouldn't have been much of a covert operation if it was all neatly recorded in the shipping logs.

However, Hudson had found something else on the datapad that he hadn't expected. When Morphus had interacted with the device, it had done more than merely counteract the station's security lock-down. It had also inadvertently unlocked access to New Providence's entire database. Including, crucially, the dealings of the Council.

There was nothing especially incriminating. The information had been logged in such a way that it sounded perfectly innocuous. However, nestled in amongst the mass of data, had been a clue to Liberty's fate. Her name was set against an entry that merely said, 'In Processing. Transfer approved.' Hudson could only guess at what this actually meant, but the chances were that Liberty was already no longer on New Providence. And he had no idea where to look next.

There was a commotion across the other side of the bar, and Hudson wondered if another card shark was causing trouble. He glanced over to see a group of patrons huddled around an epaper, chatting excitedly.

Hudson frowned, and caught Roy's attention. "What's going on over there?"

Roy sidled back over in front of Hudson, smiling. "Big news; someone has found another new portal, way out by Sapphire Alpha."

Hudson jumped off his stool, as if a thousand volts had just flowed through the seat. "Sapphire Alpha, are you sure?"

Roy nodded. "It's all over the news. Same big-ass surge of Shaak radiation, just like when they found the one near Phobos."

Hudson's hand clenched the glass of Bourbon more tightly, then he slammed it down on the table, spilling some of the liquor onto the bar. *I've got you now, you bastard! I've got you now...* he told himself, feeling the vitality return to his bones. Logan Griff had just shot up a flare, and now he knew exactly where to find him.

"You okay, Mr. Powell?" said Roy, seeming to be genuinely concerned.

Hudson drank down the rest of the Bourbon, and patted Roy on the shoulder. "Not by a parsec, but I think I'm going to be." Then he turned away and headed for the door.

"Hey, where are you going?" Roy called after him. "You haven't paid for your drink yet."

"Put it on my tab," Hudson called out. "I'll be back."

"You don't have a tab!" Roy called after him, but Hudson had already pushed through the doors. It was true that he had no idea where Liberty had been taken, but he'd bet money that Griff did. And he was going to make Cutler Wendell and Logan Griff tell him where she was, one way or another.

He'd take back what they'd stolen, and leave them with nothing.

Hudson continued to march along the corridor, back to the Orion. If there was one thing he'd learned since becoming a relic hunter, it was that he didn't want to do it alone. He was fired up, determined, and scared as hell, but he was going to find Liberty Devan, if it was the last thing he did.

The end.

EPILOGUE

Goliath completed its passage through yet another portal, emerging into a dense asteroid field in a system it had visited twice before. The first time had been to seed it. The second had been to annihilate the life it had planted there. However, this system was now merely another stepping stone on its journey to complete its task.

The portal snapped shut, creating a massive spatial distortion that rippled through the void surrounding the great ship. Asteroids in the neighboring area were torn apart like ice cubes smashed with a hammer. The ripple extended out towards the once-inhabited third planet and its moon. The surfaces of both quaked violently as the distortion passed, shaking down what little remained of their once great cities.

Goliath's pursuit of the crystal's signal had been relentless. Then, for a moment the signal had gone.

Angered at the thought that it had again been thwarted in its task, Goliath had vented its fury on another long-dead moon, cracking it across its equator like an egg. Then without explanation the signal had returned, closer than ever, and finally within its reach. In the eons since the great ship had been banished, Goliath had wandered aimlessly across the galaxy. Yet soon it would arrive at its final destination.

Furthermore, like a shark smelling blood, Goliath had also detected corporeal life, though it was beyond the realm of system 5118208. The seed of the corporeals from that world had spread, and Goliath would deal with them first.

In just two more jumps the extermination could begin. And this time, Goliath vowed that it would emerge triumphant.

TO BE CONTINUED

The Star Scavenger Series continues in book four, Union's End.

Union's End:

READ THE OTHER BOOKS IN THE SERIES:

- Guardian Outcast
- Orion Rises
- Goliath Emerges
- Union's End
- The Last Revocater

ALSO BY THIS AUTHOR

If you enjoyed this book, please consider reading The Contingency War Series, also by G J Ogden, available from Amazon and free to read for Kindle Unlimited subscribers. Also available as an audiobook on Amazon, Audible and iTunes.

- The Contingency
- The Waystation Gambit
- Rise of Nimrod Fleet
- Earth's Last War

"Highly recommended - sci-fi fans will not be disappointed with this novel."
Readers' Favorite, 5-star review.

No-one comes in peace. Every being in the galaxy wants something, and is willing to take it by force...

ABOUT THE AUTHOR

At school I was asked to write down the jobs I wanted to do as a 'grown up'. Number one was astronaut and number two was a PC games journalist. I only managed to achieve one of those goals (I'll let you guess which), but these two very different career options still neatly sum up my lifelong interests in science, space and the unknown.

School also steered me in the direction of a science-focused education over literature and writing, which influenced my decision to study physics at Manchester University. What this degree taught me is that I didn't like studying physics and instead enjoyed writing, which is why you're reading this book! The lesson? School can't tell you who you are.

When not writing, I enjoy spending time with my family, walking in the British countryside, and indulging in as much Sci-Fi as possible.

You can connect with me here:
https://twitter.com/GJ_Ogden
https://www.facebook.com/TheContingency
War

Subscribe to my newsletter:
http://subscribe.ogdenmedia.net

Printed in Great Britain
by Amazon